LITTLE SOULS

LITTLE SOULS

MICHAEL R. ZOMBER

Little Souls

For information about this title or to order other books and/or electronic media, contact the publisher:

Michael R. Zomber
mzomber@icloud.com

ISBN: 979-8-9863670-0-2

Printed in the United States of America

"He that kills another's ox, sins, not through killing the ox,
but through injuring another man in his property."

~ Thomas Aquinas: Summa Theologica, 1274

"One day, we will see our animals again in the eternity
of Christ. Paradise is open to all God's creatures."

~ Pope Francis: 2014

Contents

CHAPTER 1

An Unhappy Family
in Retrospect

Charles Dickens begins his *A Tale of Two Cities* with: "It was the best of times, it was the worst of times . . ." In the Sanders's home it was never the best of times and all too often the worst. My father Ted was still fighting the Civil War, or as he always called it: "The War of the Northern Aggression." If I ever referred to the conflict as the Civil War, he would immediately begin to rant and rave about "those goddamned Yankee schoolbooks and carpetbagging, Northern, nigger-loving teachers who don't know a damned thing about history." If I were lucky he would limit his corrective measures to words. Unfortunately, all too often my understandable mistake lead to my being boxed on either the left or right ear or both one after the other. These were hard slaps that would deafen me for a few minutes besides being really painful. What was really bad was when my mom defended me saying that I was trying to be an American

and not just a Southerner and that the War, whatever one wanted to call it had been over since 1865.

When I was eleven we lived in a large plantation home that had housed generations of Sanders since before the Civil War. There had been some improvements made since such as flush toilets and hot water plumbing and other conveniences, which were installed by my paternal great-grandfather, Josiah Sanders, who had made a good deal of money during Prohibition selling his corn and rye to several local stills whose whiskey was well regarded by the locals and Northerners alike. By the time I was born, my father had spent almost all of great-grandpa's money and the men who had worked in our fields had almost all migrated to the big cities in search of better pay and, more important, to escape Jim Crow.

The walls of the great room were covered with framed steel engravings of Robert E. Lee, Stonewall Jackson, P.G.T. Beauregard, and my father's hero, Nathan Bedford Forest. Of course there was no portrait of General James Longstreet whom Dad regarded as "The Judas of the South" and a "race traitor" primarily because in 1874 he led black troops against the White League in New Orleans. Above the large stone fireplace hung a genuine Confederate flag rescued by an ancestor after the disastrous Battle of Nashville when Union forces under General George Thomas, the Rock of Chickamauga, routed John Bell Hood's army. My ancestor fought with General Stephen Lee, whose courageous rear guard action saved Hood's forces from total annihilation. Additionally there was a curio cabinet filled with medals, kepis, a nine-shot LeMat revolver, and a Southern Navy Colt, a Leech and Rigdon, I think. Resting on a hand-carved walnut rack were several cavalry sabers with fancy guards bearing the initials CS and CSA, together with two long muskets and one carbine either brought back from the War or carried in it by some ancient Sanders.

By the time I turned eleven, the outside of the house was a cacophony of peeling white paint, porch railings both second floor and ground level missing enough pickets to make them hazardous and look like the grinning mouths of Halloween jack-o'-lanterns. The stove in our cavernous kitchen was new during Franklin Roosevelt's third term. The Doric columns that once stood so proudly were weathered, split and the left one leaned to one side precariously supporting the upper porch. Lacking central heat, much less air conditioning, in winter my bedroom was cold and in summer, especially in August, stiflingly hot. Dad had bought us some space heaters from the Sears Roebuck in Memphis and my parent's bedroom had a window air conditioner that you could hear groaning throughout the second floor.

There were rooms that were closed off, full of old High Point and Thomasville sofas with rusty and broken springs poking through the horsehair and velvet; chairs with three legs, broken cane seats, broken backs; Turkish carpets worn through with holes; more ruby glassware than you could imagine; the depressing decrepit trappings of an upper class, genteel Southern existence now relegated to our numerous lumber rooms. There was an attic equally filled with discards that had seen better days in great-grandfather's time but I never went up there. The folding, pull-down stairs were missing several steps and the coil springs were much too strong for me to pull. The only time I dared follow Dad up I saw stuffed deer heads and other creepy things staring at me with their glassy dead eyes and a cobweb stretching from the dormer to one of the heads that looked thick enough to entangle me so I would never escape. I didn't see its arachnid author and I had no desire to.

My mom was in her fiftieth year when I was eleven. She was the daughter of a wealthy and respected Charleston family. She met my dad at a Confederate Costume Ball held by The United Daughters of the Confederacy

at the Jefferson Hotel in Richmond. They had a lovely Southern wedding in Charleston. I know because I passed by the framed pictures in the hall every day. They were happy for at least one year as far as I know but then it was all downhill from there. Dad spent most of his inheritance keeping up all the appearances of a landed aristocrat and shortly after my fifth birthday money became tight and only got tighter with each succeeding year. Dad's drinking increased in an inverse ratio with his capital. The arguments between Mom and Dad increased in frequency and intensity as each blamed the other for the situation. She blamed his drinking and he blamed her family for failing to support them financially. The big John Deere 530 tractor, once bright green and yellow and my father's pride, now red with rust and a flat rear tire, lay nearly buried by tall weeds near our dilapidated, clapboard barn.

I remember my beautiful mom looking tired, a veritable flock of crow's-feet clustering around her once bright, sky blue eyes. She had given up trying to dress nicely. I guess when lunch consisted of Jif peanut butter on Bunny Bread six days a week and boiled potatoes, and greens, with a few bits of pork for dinner six days a week, she thought why bother keeping up appearances when sitting down for supper?

One crisp autumn afternoon, I think it was a Saturday, or maybe it was during the week and school was canceled because of Columbus Day or Veteran's Day I don't remember. Dad and I were riding home in his Cadillac El Dorado convertible, the one thing we owned that he took scrupulous care of. Every Sunday he would wash that car and rub the paint with Turtle Wax it until his arm got tired and then he would open that red, white, and blue tin can of Nevr-Dull and polish the chrome so bright that when the sun hit the bumpers it was like a mirror that would blind you. He religiously treated the blue leather seats with LEXOL® as if anointing them so they always smelled what he liked to call "showroom fresh" and looked as good as the day he brought it home.

Damn it. I lied. It must have been what they call a Freudian slip. There was one other thing on the Sanders plantation that Dad regarded with even more love and reverence than his El Dorado. That was the six-by-ten foot, wool Confederate flag that flew atop the thirty-foot high aluminum pole in the very middle of the circular gravel area in front of our house. Dad would carefully raise it up when he rose in the morning and lower it when the sun began to set each evening. He would bring it into the dining room and fold it as carefully as any United States marines ever folded an American flag to present to the widow or child of a fallen comrade. This invariable habit never bothered me much as a child but as soon as I understood exactly what it represented, just seeing it fluttering in our drive gave me the same sick feeling in my stomach that the stuffed heads in the attic once did.

I was in the front seat next to dad listening to Hank Williams Jr. on the local country radio station singing "A Country Boy Can Survive." Dad was singing along quietly and I was humming along. The tires were making a pleasant crunching sound on the gravel of our driveway. We had just turned in off the paved road, past the weathered white Sanders Plantation sign, when my dad saw something by the side of the drive. He twitched the steering wheel fast to the right and I heard a thump and a thin, high-pitched scream. He drove on about the length of the car and slammed the brakes on so hard I knocked my head on the padded dash. It was near dusk and he opened his door and was getting out as I opened mine to see what he'd hit on purpose.

A beautiful raccoon was struggling, dark blood on its snout. I screamed. "Daddy! You hurt him." I ran to the raccoon and bent over him.

"Leave him be."

I was about to pick him up and hold him.

"Stephanie, I'm serious. I said don't touch him. Might be rabid. You stay right here. I'll be back."

I watched him walk off then I reached down and spoke to the raccoon.

"I'm so sorry. I'll pray for you."

I began to pray and ask God to fix the raccoon.

"Please don't let him die. He's so beautiful"

The raccoon grunted softly as if he heard me. I don't know if it made him feel any better but the big lump in my throat began to dissolve.

"I'm sorry. I know you must hurt something awful. Daddy will be right back. Then you'll be okay. I promise."

When Ted reached the house he stomped in, and glared at Laura, who was boiling potatoes. Steam was rising from the aluminum Dutch oven.

"I finally got the damn raccoon that's been digging in the trash." There was a distinct note of triumph in his tone as if he'd done some glorious deed.

Laura grunted dispiritedly. "Uh-huh."

Ted walked to a corner of his private den where there was an old oak gun cabinet with a lever action Winchester Model 1894, a Winchester Model 1897 pump 12 gauge shotgun, and a WWII M1 Garand standing upright. He crouched and opened the drawer at the bottom of the rack and removed a venerable, six-inch, pencil barrel, .22 caliber Colt Woodsman automatic pistol with most of the blue worn off. He carefully drew back the slide and saw there was already a round in the chamber. He thumbed on the safety. With a look of pleasurable anticipation on his normally grim face he left through the kitchen without a look or a word. Seeing her husband, pistol in hand, Laura made a face so full of disgust and utter disdain that had Ted seen it there would have been some serious trouble. As it was she continued to chop greens and mince pork with increasingly agitated knife strokes as if she would have preferred to mince her husband.

As I hovered over the stricken raccoon Dad approached with the pistol in his right hand at his side, the barrel pointing down. He spoke in a commanding tone.

"Stand aside."

At first I obeyed and retreated a few steps. Then I abruptly jumped forward shielding the raccoon. I pleaded in between taking short, almost asthmatic breaths.

"Daddy, we can fix him. I know it. Please don't shoot him. Please daddy. Please."

Hot tears streamed down my reddened and contorted face. Ted's face was flushing as his anger rose. He was not accustomed to being thwarted and defied by Laura, much less by me, his only child. Still, knowing my defiant nature he tried to soften his previous tone and spoke more quietly.

"Stephanie, I told you to stand aside."

I began to shake. As he continued watching his daughter defying him, Ted's rage mounted. Torn between my overwhelming need to protect the wounded animal and knowing all too well from previous experience the punishing consequences attendant on disobedience, usually administered with his thick, broad, brown leather belt and that is if I were lucky. I was acquainted not just with the pain of the leather but also with the agony caused by the heavy brass buckle bearing the raised C.S.A. initials that held up father's blue denim trousers. As he raised the pistol he spoke with a menace I knew all too well. His voice was even more of a snarl than it usually was when he felt he was not being given the proper respect he thought was due him.

"I won't ask you a third time. Now git or else!"

There was no need for Ted to explain the meaning of "or else." Ted glared at me as if he would have liked to shoot me instead of the raccoon or better still both of us. It was too terrifying to contemplate and shaking ever more violently I moved away with a lurch. The crack of a high velocity .22 split the otherwise quiet evening as I shrieked.

"No Daddy. No!" The raccoon lay still. I looked my father in the eye, then at the thin curl of smoke from the muzzle of the pistol and only then

at the dead animal with an oozing red hole where once there had been an eye. I bent over and retched violently again and again as Ted looked away utterly disgusted.

Once I finished retching, daddy grabbed my right arm, twisted it behind my back and frog-marched me to the car. He opened the passenger door and shoved me in. He'd said nothing while he was pushing me, then he growled.

"If you puke in my car you'll wish you hadn't."

I was still feeling sick in my stomach, sore in my throat, and worse, I was hurting deep down in my heart. I was on the verge of asking God to kill my father and resurrect the raccoon like Jesus brought Lazarus back from the dead but I bit back that thought and said nothing. Mom was leaning out the door looking at us. She sagged against one pillar and said in a tired voice,

"You two best come in and wash for supper."

Dinner was an even cheerless affair than usual and none of us said much I can remember. I excused myself and went up to my bedroom. I lay down on the bed and pulled the fluffy feather pillow over my face to muffle my sobs. I heard the front door open, then I got up and went to the window to look out. It was not yet full dark and I saw daddy carrying a heavy plastic bag and drop it into one of the dented, steel trashcans. Our old quarter horse, Robert Lee, chuffed a little at the commotion, then returned to cropping the brown grass in the pasture. I heard the crash of the lid being slammed down.

Ted was still furious as he returned from dumping the raccoon in the trash. He stomped to the big, stained, white porcelain farm sink in which Laura was rinsing the dinner dishes. He nudged her aside and commenced to vigorously washing his hands in the hot soapy water. Laura stood to the side considering what to say for a moment.

"Ted, lately it seems to me that you're only really happy when you're killing something."

Ted dried his hands on a ragged cotton towel. His face reddened slightly.

"Laura, I'd really appreciate it if just for once you'd show me the respect the good Lord commands you to show. Set an example of a God-fearing woman for Stephanie instead of always undermining my authority in my own house."

Laura replied with bitter sarcasm in a tone that spoke of long years of dominant male psychological oppression and at more than a few times, physical correction.

"Well you just set a great example." She added perhaps unnecessarily: "As usual."

Ted, who was on the way to his den and his habitual evening appointment with Jim Beam or Jack Daniel's, wheeled and rounded on Laura. He shouted.

"Dammit Laura. I am fed up to here with your lip and your high-minded bullshit."

He took a deep breath.

"I'll tell you what. How about you go back to Charleston and that fine old family you're always bragging on and reminding me that Sanders is nothing compared to McIver and that your grandfather was a U.S. senator crap. Last time we saw them they made me like some field nigger asking massa for permission to go into town."

"Just because poppa wouldn't give you fifty thousand dollars. What were you going to do with it? Buy a new Cadillac? Restore Sanders Plantation? We never discussed it. You just expected Poppa to write you a check? After all he's already given us?"

"I've had it with you and Stephanie. The two of you can just go away. At least I'll have some peace. Then maybe for once I can build a life worth living."

Laura hissed.

"Leave Stephanie out of this, Ted. She has nothing to do with it. Show me the type of class you had at the ball the evening we met. You were another man then. This miserable life we lead is not the one you promised me."

Ted calmed down and whined. "You and your spoiled brat daughter have ruined my life. If only you'd given me a son, a Sanders's son and heir, things would be different and you know it."

Laura's voice rose to a shriek. I heard it and walked quietly to the stairs to listen more carefully.

"That is so unfair. You claim to believe in the God that determines everything in your life. If God wanted you to have a son then you would have one."

Ted snarled.

"Don't remind me. Every day the sun goes down I feel it setting on the Sanders's line. The Sanders name dies with me."

Laura muttered softly under her breath so Ted couldn't hear.

"The sooner the better."

Ted stormed out of the kitchen.

Laura spoke audibly to the fast retreating figure. "God may forgive you Ted Sanders but I never will."

I tiptoed back up the stairs carefully avoiding the one next to the top step, which sometimes creaked loudly if anyone stepped on it wrong. I opened the second drawer of the pine nightstand and took out an old Rayovac metal flashlight and switched it on. The beam illuminated the numerous posters of various animals especially horses. I opened the dormer window with great care and climbed out onto the porch then climbed down the lattice that screened that part of the porch. As I approached the trashcan a raccoon ran from the beam cast by the Rayovac and startled me. Through the unshaded den window I could see my father cleaning his pistol. Lifting the trashcan lid as gently as I could, I eased the heavy plastic bag from the can. It rattled slightly from the weight and the faint sound caused Ted to stop oiling the Woodsman for a moment. He listened than put down the pistol and took up a briar pipe and lit it with his old Zippo lighter. He took several puffs then picked up the Colt to return it to its drawer.

I heaved the plastic bag over my right shoulder. I stopped for a moment as the horse trotted over expecting a treat.

"I'm sorry Mr. Lee but I got to get over to George's. I'll make it up to you tomorrow after breakfast, I promise."

The horse snorted softly and I raced off barefoot through the pasture.

I didn't care about stepping in Mr. Lee's road apples with my bare feet. I just had to get to George's house before anyone started looking for me, particularly my dad. George's is not much more than a big, one-room cabin, but I like it a lot more than Sanders Plantation. There is a little sign by the front porch that says, "George and Faith." Faith is George's wife. They are black and George is older than my dad but they get along way better than my mom and dad. They don't have any children but they don't seem to mind. Besides they always say I'm like the daughter they always dreamt of. Daddy does not much like me spending too much time with George. He says they are trash and the only reason they live on their own land is that his father made the mistake of selling George's father ten acres. But even daddy has to say George is honest and he does work hard for him when he needs a hand so he just doesn't want me speaking like black people do. I was out of breath from carrying the raccoon and set the bag down on the porch. I rapped on the thin, yellow pine door with the round, brass doorknob.

Inside the modest room George Jackson looked at his gold-filled Elgin railroad pocket watch. He glanced from the watch's white enamel dial over to the wheelchair draped with a crocheted shawl then walked to the door.

"Stevie Sanders, what brings you out at this time of night, barefoot and breathing hard. Your daddy do something to you?"

I just stood there, tears rolling down my face. I opened the plastic bag and George looked inside.

"Daddy shot him dead. He ran him over on purpose then he shot him."

"Hush now, child. You'll wake Mrs. Jackson."

"But he did it all on purpose. I hate him. I wish he was dead."

With that I began to cry in earnest. My thin body was wracked with sobs and the shakes. George nodded slowly and opened his muscular arms wide. I rushed to him and he cradled me, whispering softly.

"Now, now child, we'll see to him properly."

In the center of the Sanders Plantation slave cemetery was a ruined slave shack used for storage. The rudimentary weathered granite stones were chiseled with the names of various African American Jacksons. Each grave as well as the entire cemetery was enclosed by a low white picket fence in varying stages of decay and discoloration. Illuminated by the light of a green Coleman gas lantern we stood next to a mound of newly dug earth and a miniature open grave. George took two slats from a nearly picket fence and wired them together with bailing wire to form a cross. He gently tapped the marker into the dirt at the head of the grave with the side of an old mattock.

We prayed over the grave with the plastic bag resting at the foot.

George spoke the lines from the end of Coleridge's "Rime of the Ancient Mariner":

"He prayeth well who loveth well
Both man and bird and beast."

He continued.

"He prayeth best who loveth best
All things, both great and small:
For the dear God who loveth us,
He made and loveth all."

"That's all I remember of that poem. I used to know it all by heart."

I said, "That's got to be the best part."

"Now you best be getting on home before there's trouble."

George filled in the grave as I walked away quickly. Then George shouldered the mattock and walked slowly home.

CHAPTER 2

Theological Dispute
Genesis

The schoolhouse was a one-story, red brick building with no air conditioning. Consequently the mostly dirt playground, encircled by a three-foot high cyclone fence was the children's respite from the heat and was fully occupied at every legal opportunity. Stephanie was not as well-dressed as some others with greater pretensions to gentility and she was wearing a fairly clean white shirt and a cotton skirt. At age twelve, she was tall and thin with runner's legs, shoulder-length, straight, dirty blond hair; a thoughtful but pleasing face with regular features; a few scattered freckles, light blue eyes, and tan skin from spending much time outdoors in the sun. Seemingly oblivious to the happy shouts and cries from her schoolmates, Stephanie stood apart staring up at the clouds and ciphering as many animal shapes, both real and imaginary, as she could. Her textbooks were covered with craft paper and festooned with stickers

14

of her favorite creatures, mainly horses of different breeds and interspersed here and there with a German shepherd or collie dog.

She was absorbed in a reverie when a football landed at her feet with a thump, startling her.

"Stephanie!"

The voice came from Daniel Olsen who had been tossing the ball to his older brother Luke. Daniel was eleven, and already marked out by the teachers and the Zion community for a confirmed rascal with a shaggy shock of dark red hair, a stocky build, flashing hazel eyes, and a quizzical smile that rarely left his thin lips without a grin. His teachers loved him and he skated out of situations that would have landed any other boy in detention or worse, the dreaded office of Mrs. Sonnen, the spinsterish, sixty-year-old assistant principal, whose opinion of troublesome students was similar to W.C. Fields. When asked how he liked children Fields replied, "I like children. If they're properly cooked." Luke Olsen was twelve and already looked as if he were carrying the weight of the world on his shoulders. He was tall, with short black hair, almost ascetically thin but with a handsome face framed by thick dark eyebrows. There were dark shadows under his eyes as if sleep came to him with difficulty. Luke was a frequent denizen of study hall detention as math and social studies did not appeal to him. The Olsen boys, as people referred to them, were very little alike either in appearance or behavior but they were best friends notwithstanding. Their father was the highly respected sheriff of the county and their mother had died following an agonizingly protracted and excruciating bout with breast cancer when they were nine and ten respectively. Daniel picked up the ball and looked directly at Stephanie.

"Heard you got in trouble with Mr. Hall."

John Hall was the social studies teacher, a straight-laced Southern Baptist with a round, florid face, a broad flabby butt, a medium paunch,

and little tolerance for anything he viewed as heterodoxy both religious and secular either in or out of the classroom. He had married young and exuded a distinct aura of disappointment in his relations with both his wife and his students. Mr. Hall was easily offended by student's questions and had sent more of his charges to detention and to Mrs. Sonnen than any two other teachers combined.

Stephanie was still absorbed in a cumulus cloud that resembled a dragon and her tone was neutral, though, in truth, she found Luke's brooding presence attractive.

"I did?"

"You told Hall that animals have souls like we do?"

Mr. Hall occasionally tried to give his students religious instruction and that afternoon he read from the King James Bible Matthew 10:28. "And fear not them which kill the body, but are not able to kill the soul:"

Stephanie had raised her hand and asked,

"What about the animals?"

Mr. Hall looked at her severely and said, "Thomas Aquinas clearly demonstrates that animals do not have souls."

Stephanie replied, "Thomas Aquinas is wrong."

"Stephanie Sanders how dare you question not only me but Thomas Aquinas? You speak blasphemy! You go to Mrs. Sonnen's office right now!"

Luke was incredulous and his raised eyebrows echoed his disbelief that she had the audacity to contradict Hall whom he thought was a pompous bully and a mean-spirited, petty tyrant.

"You told Hall that animals have souls like we do? That they go to heaven just like us?

"They certainly do and they certainly will."

Daniel said, "They don't."

Stephanie glared at the brothers.

"Do too! God gives each one of them their own little soul."

Luke turned from Stephanie to look at Daniel then back at her.

"Did Black George tell you that?"

"His name is George Jackson and yes he did, skinny, white, pimple-face Luke."

At that moment a large black Ford pickup truck emblazoned with a gold star seal on the driver's door reading, "Sheriff's Department Clark County" pulled up.

Sheriff Olsen dressed in full uniform rolled down the window.

"Let's go boys. It's time."

Reluctant to leave such an interesting discussion yet knowing that his father did not like to be kept waiting, Daniel looked at Luke.

"C'mon Luke."

Abashed at Stephanie's fierce reaction to his description of George Jackson Luke sought to make amends. Ignoring the butterflies of shame flitting in his stomach he said somewhat hopefully.

"See ya 'round, Stephanie."

Her face flushed with annoyance at the perceived lack of respect the brothers showed her best friend, George, and in spite of her attraction toward Luke, she said acidly:

"In your dreams, maybe."

The passenger door slammed and as the sheriff's truck drove off Luke turned to look through the rear window at Stephanie. Her sad expression touched a sore place in his own broken heart and his eyes filled with unshed tears.

CHAPTER 3

Death of a Deputy

Luke Olsen, thirty-two, stood in his underwear, smoking a Marlboro Light, staring at the beige Zion Sheriff's Department uniform in the open, mirrored, cheap coat closet in a roadside motel. The once white, blown-in cottage cheese ceiling was smoke darkened, the bed with the faux walnut, pressed wood headboard was deeply scratched with some peeling veneer mostly at the edges. The olive green nylon polyester carpet was pockmarked here and there with cigarette craters and unidentifiable dark stains. Luke was 6 foot and weighed 150 pounds. He had recently lost weight due to a steady diet of Wild Turkey and a daily order of $3.99 Cajun Double Steakburger 'n Fries. His otherwise attractive face was pale, accented by the pronounced dark circles and bags under his brown eyes. He walked closer to the mirror and studied himself. Then he walked to the brown Formica veneered nightstand topped with a nearly empty fifth

18

of Jim Beam and a framed six-by-eight wedding photo, in which appeared a younger fitter Luke with a lovely, lissome, small-breasted, blond woman in her twenties with a smiling face and startlingly green eyes framed by a bell of natural blond, shoulder-length, wavy hair. Luke's best man dressed in a white rented tuxedo with scruffy unkempt red hair and a five-day growth of beard looked on with a slightly bemused expression, a faint smile playing on his lips.

Luke picked up the bottle of Jim Beam, tilted it up and drank the last inch of the bourbon. He removed a black leather badge case from his right side jeans pocket and contemplated the bright gold-and-enamel star for several minutes with a rueful expression. He removed the shield from the case, placing it carefully next to a beige manila envelope. Opening the drawer of the nightstand he took the motel pen and with his right hand trembling, shakily wrote in block capital letters: "FOR DANIEL" on the envelope. Then Luke took his duty weapon, a Sig Sauer P 226 nine-millimeter automatic pistol, from under the pillow. He carefully pulled back the slide to make certain there was a round in the chamber. Walking slowly like an automaton in a nightmare, he made his way to the bathroom. Once inside, he closed the door and sat down on the stained white plastic lid of the porcelain toilet. Luke placed the muzzle of the Sig under his chin and resolutely pulled the double-action trigger.

Daniel Olsen drove north on I-65 toward Zion as Peterbilt, Volvo, and other sparkling and massive eighteen-wheel semitrailers passed him at more than seventy miles per hour. One chrome cab-over monster nearly pushed his old red Ford F-150 onto the shoulder. Passing the gray, blue, and white "Tennessee The Volunteer State Welcomes You" sign, Daniel continued on to his exit, then on to a two-lane country road past fields, ponds, and creeks until he came to a small white-and-black sign reading "Zion 3 miles." Slowing down to twenty miles per hour as the potholes

in the asphalt became more and more numerous, he glanced at the half-opened leather badge case on the truck's seat containing a New Orleans police shield.

Stephanie's well-loved and well worn, beige Toyota pick-up truck lay parked on the grassy shoulder of the road, the emergency lights flashing. The truck bed was filled with a canvas pup tent and various paraphernalia including a large aluminum water cooler. The front and rear bumpers bore stickers reading "Love Animals, Don't Eat Them." Painted on the driver's door was a vignette of a cocker spaniel and a calico tabby cat at play and above it in black Gothic script letters "Little Souls" above a telephone number. Stephanie, now a pretty woman just turned thirty, was gently ministering to the crushed remains of a horned owl. As she placed it in a white plastic bag, Daniel's Ford with Louisiana plates pulled up behind her. He opened the door and stepped out, carefully scanning the ground and studying the woman holding the plastic bag.

"Stephanie, Stephanie Sanders, is that you?"

Still holding the bag Stephanie looked him over.

"Daniel."

She rose to face him, a thin smile on her face.

"You've been away a long time. By the way, folks around here all call me Stevie now. I like it better and so do they. Steph just sounds too much like staph."

"I see you're still ministering to stricken and dead creatures."

Stevie nodded then said in a tone filled with genuine sorrow:

"Really sorry about your brother."

Daniel's face darkened, the guilt on his face clear as could be, mixed with shame. His voice was shaky and an octave higher than usual.

"I didn't see Luke much these past few years. Been working down in New Orleans."

"Uh-huh. You kinda just disappeared."

Daniel looked at his stainless steel wristwatch.

"Sorry but I gotta run."

"You gonna stay in town for a while?"

Stevie climbed into her truck and placed the owl bag next to the child's car seat strapped with the passenger seat belt. She turned the key and started the motor. Stevie leaned out the driver's window. Daniel looked at her appraisingly and said softly:

"I don't really know."

Stevie replied with real feeling:

"I'm sorry. I really and truly am."

"Be seeing you, Steph, I mean Stevie."

"I hope so. It's good to see you, Daniel."

Daniel forced a smile as Stevie drove off. He watched her Toyota disappear around a bend in the road.

CHAPTER 4

A Funeral

To say Pastor Peter was uneasy in his mind would be a masterpiece of understatement. He knew the reasons for Luke Olsen's suicide all too well and though he was not in the least responsible, he still felt guilty. His knowing every reason behind the act, coupled with the fact that Luke and he had been friends were like a lead weight in his heart. He felt he had failed in practicing and exemplifying genuine Christianity as both pastor of the Zion Baptist Church and Luke's spiritual advisor. If only he had addressed Luke's long, slow, stately decline into alcoholism and depression in a more direct manner rather than sharing the occasional beer with him at the tavern. True, he had sympathized and empathized with Luke's issues but seemingly insoluble relationship conundrums of his own made him feel inadequate, like the proverbial whited sepulcher when they were together. As far as he knew

Luke was a damned good law enforcement officer and he had heard few if any complaints about him from his parishioners, even the ones he had arrested for domestic abuse or driving under the influence. Of course, his father was the county sheriff, but it seemed that had no effect on Luke's professionalism. He knew the root cause of Luke's depression, as did nearly every other resident of Zion over the age of twelve and probably some who were no more than six.

Luke's funeral was held on a Sunday afternoon. The Zion Baptist church was a typical small town church building with white painted wood sides, a white cross on the pitched roof, and a spartan interior with oak pews and matching lectern. Pastor Peter was finishing the oration.

"Gracious Lord, accept our prayers for the salvation of the soul of Your humble servant, Lucas Olaf Olsen."

Sheriff Robert Olsen stood quietly, resplendent in his full dress uniform, his Desert Storm combat ribbons and Bronze Star adorning his left breast. As Pastor Peter's words echoed through the church, Daniel walked in. The mourners turned to look at the latecomer. Sheriff Olsen saw his son and forced a thin smile of acknowledgment.

Peter continued, "And grant him entrance into the land of everlasting light and peace where there is no more pain or sorrow, through the grace of our Lord Jesus Christ. Amen."

The mourners gathered by a newly dug grave in the small cemetery. The volunteer sexton had first removed the grass by hand, carefully laying the turf in layers so it could be replaced on the mound once the grave had been refilled. Using a red, subcompact Kubota backhoe, he had scooped out the grave with minimal damage to the surrounding gravesites. Luke's simple pine casket from Trappist Caskets rested on a bier. Sheriff Olsen, assisted by Duncan Hunter, Daniel, and three other members of the congregation lifted the coffin from the bier then using ropes gently lowered it into the

grave. Duncan Hunter handed the sheriff a bolt action 1903 Springfield army rifle and three blank cartridges. The sheriff loaded the cartridges into the magazine then shouldered the rifle, closed the bolt and fired three shots in close succession as Daniel stood rigid, hand frozen to his forehead in a salute. The assembly dispersed as the echo of the 30–06 blanks faded and a wisp of smoke hovered above Luke's grave. The sheriff nodded formally to his only remaining son and left with Duncan in the patrol car. Pastor Peter joined with the others leaving Daniel standing stone-faced, silent, and alone beside his brother's grave.

A Different Funeral

Stevie Sanders mounded fresh earth on a newly dug and very small grave. Using a small shovel she carefully tapped a small, white painted, simple cross into the grass at the head of the grave. The cross itself was unmarked, the occupant of the grave anonymous. She stood, slightly stiff from squatting, and dusted earth from her jeans. She walked to her pickup and put the shovel in the bed. Turning, she surveyed the cemetery and the hundreds of miniature, white crosses that dotted the landscape surrounding the dilapidated slave shack that stood in the center. The view always put her in mind of the pictures of Flanders Field American Cemetery in Belgium with its white crosses and John McCrae's poem: "In Flanders fields the poppies blow. Between the crosses, row on row." Stevie would have liked poppies but her cemetery was run on an oftentimes less than the proverbial shoestring budget.

The white sign with black medieval Gothic lettering arching over the entry reading "LITTLE SOULS" had been extravagant enough and forced her to postpone a much needed lube, oil, and filter service for her Toyota.

George Jackson rode up on his battered, blue John Deere pulling a red wagon occupied by a five year old who could have passed for Stevie at that age assuming Stevie had had light brown hair. Gigi leapt from the wagon before it stopped, landed nimbly on her feet, and raced to her mother who scooped her up. Stevie admonished her in a not unkindly tone.

"How many times have I told you not to jump from a moving vehicle?"

"I didn't jump from the tractor. I jumped from the wagon."

"I know. I saw you."

Knowing this admonition was a loser Stevie said enthusiastically: "How's my Gigi?"

Gigi looked at the fresh grave.

"Who's buried there?"

"A cottontail rabbit."

Gigi's little face darkened and tears glistened in her gray eyes.

"A bunny?"

"I'm afraid so. But she's at rest now and her little soul is with God."

George parked the tractor in the gravel driveway in front of his farmhouse. He shut off the engine and dismounted somewhat painfully. He walked to Stevie while Gigi looked for some wildflowers to place on the bunny's grave.

"You've been gone quite some time."

"I saw Daniel Olsen. He came back because of his brother."

Stevie's voice trailed off.

"It's a terrible sad thing when a young person takes his own life. And if I recollect rightly you and Daniel were . . ."

Before George could finish his sentence Stevie cut him off rather more sharply than she intended to and with a tone that was more acid than she had ever used with George. It contained equal parts frustration, bitterness, and anger leavened with a strong dose of sorrow and regret.

"We weren't anything because when we were in high school his daddy, the sheriff, kept us from ever being together. Even back then his father thought I was an animal-loving loony. He made sure Daniel and Luke shot their first deer as soon as they could lift and sight a 30–30 and kill anything that walked or crawled whether it was with a gun or a boot. Once I saw Luke stomp a garter snake to death. Both boys were mean to animals thanks to their dad."

Stevie was about to cry just thinking about the snake and ran to her truck. Rather than reacting to her outburst by being offended, George knew Stevie was heart hurt by Daniel's return, Luke's suicide, and the exquisitely painful girlhood memories, which she kept carefully concealed and as she opened the door to buckle Gigi into her car seat George said soothingly:

"Us loons need to stick together. So when do I get the pleasure of having supper under my roof for a change with you and Gigi?"

Mollified by George's gentle reply though still hurt, Stevie spoke quietly.

"Be careful of what you wish for. One day soon the two of us might just move in permanently."

George smiled as Stevie came around and opened the driver's door. George closed the door and leaned on the window frame.

"Nothing I'd like better. You know since my Faith passed I get real lonely some nights. Be real nice having you two around."

Stevie leaned out and kissed him on the cheek. Gigi waved as Stevie started the truck and slowly drove off.

Daniel Olsen cruised slowly down Main Street. In the case of Zion, Main Street really was just that as there was little in the way of side streets.

He saw a sign toward the west end outside a late Victorian clapboard home. It looked clean and inviting. The sign in the front yard read, "Clean rooms for rent, Low Monthly Rates." He pulled over to the curb and opened the truck door.

Stevie had made her old Airstream trailer into a comfortable home for her and Gigi. She had painted floral murals inhabited with birds, squirrels, and rabbits, transforming the aluminum sides into works of art. Outside the trailer were redwood flower boxes filled with colorful perennials. Inside a chicken wire enclosure were two Nubian goats, seven Rhode Island Red chickens. Three Coral Blue guineas, two Blue peafowl, and two dogs of indeterminate breed all of which seemed to get along fairly well with occasional dustups and loud encounters, mostly between the peafowl and the dogs, but as yet nothing had proved fatal or even serious. Though only a few hundred yards away from the Sanders's ancestral home, Stevie's trailer seemed to be in a different world altogether. An ancient, black-and-white quarter horse grazed lazily in his small, white wooden-fenced paddock behind the trailer.

Inside the Airstream, Stevie was medicating a sick, orange billed, very overweight white duck, while she kept an eye on Gigi who was in the outside enclosure unsuccessfully attempting to ride one of the goats. The trailer walls were lined with calendars from the World Wildlife Fund and the white enamel Frigidaire refrigerator was festooned with magnets from Greenpeace, the ASPCA, and various animal welfare societies. There were glass aquaria occupied by a black racer, a painted turtle, and a large green bullfrog respectively. Stevie was answering the phone when the duck suddenly emptied his bowels with a large greenish and runny stool. At that moment Gigi rushed in screaming at the top of her lungs. Juggling the phone and avoiding contact with the duck's mess, she had no time to deal with her daughter in addition. She said breathlessly into the phone:

"No time to talk right now. I'm behind on paying for supplies. Gigi please stop! K . . . I love you too."

Pastor Peter was on his cell phone, his face illuminated by the refracted sunlight pouring through the one stained-glass window depicting Jesus as the Lamb of God.

"Give Gigi a hug and a kiss from me."

He put the phone in his pocket and looked out across the empty church.

CHAPTER 6

A Study in Contrast

The estate belonging to Lucille Abbott was nothing short of spectacular and far and away the most luxurious in the county much less Zion itself. It would have not been an outlier in the toniest part of Newport, Rhode Island, or the Hamptons. The grounds were manicured to perfection and the green of the expanse of Kentucky blue grass was vibrant, cut carefully to a height of one inch creating a veritable five-acre putting green. The circular driveway accommodated more than twenty cars and was set around a tall, polished aluminum flagpole in its own half-acre round, gently convex grassy mound. That morning, a handsome, thirty-something African American, named Zeke, short for Ezekiel, dressed in full livery, was raising the Stars and Stripes as he did every morning, weather permitting.

After he tied the thick cotton rope securely, he walked to the polished steel serving cart and began to set out the ostentatious Tiffany sterling silver coffee pot, creamer, and sugar on a gleaming white tablecloth on a mahogany folding table next to a matching mahogany Chippendale-style armchair. Lucille Abbott, a lovely woman in her fifties but looking much younger, emerged from the imposing Ionic-columned front entrance, cradling an enormous, aging tabby cat, which appeared to be almost comatose with rheumy eyes and a leaking nose. Zeke seated Lucille and looked dubiously at the cat.

"Shall I take Muffy, ma'am?

"Yes, please, she's rather heavy and feeling rather poorly today."

"One lump or two today?"

"Oh, Zeke, only one for me."

She looked down at the cat, which lay on its side breathing heavily.

"One lump for Muffy. She could use a treat."

Zeke took a lump from the sugar bowl and held it in front of Muffy's runny nose. As the treat approached, Muffy roused herself from her lethargy, sniffed and opened her mouth to receive the sweet revealing long, yellowed and carious fangs.

"There. That's better isn't it, Muffykins?"

Zeke removed a silk handkerchief from his coat pocket and wiped the feline slobber from his thumb and forefinger.

The Sanders home stood as a counterpoint to Lucille Abbott's superb residence. Nearly all the paint had peeled from the once proud columns and the columns themselves displayed large cracks and areas of rot. The drive was bordered by and patched, with tall weeds of diverse species including goldenrod, milkweed, nettles, fireweed, goosegrass, and crabgrass growing along the edges with a few thriving in the numerous ruts. The gravel itself was rutted and checkered with small washouts from thunderstorms. The once proud Stars and Bars was tattered and holed, sun faded, and the red now light pink, and the stars all but invisible. The interior of Ted's

ancestral home mirrored the dilapidation of the exterior. His pine-paneled study was actually even more depressing. Mounds of foot-high piles of yellowing newspapers dotted the holed and frayed, once lovely Aubusson carpet, formerly the pride of Ted's grandfather. The glass case holding the Sanders family swords, Richmond musket, and other Confederate relics was smudged with countless greasy fingerprints. The doors at the bottom of the wall-length mahogany bookcase were warped and one hung precariously from its hinges. The quarter calf leather-bound editions of Shakespeare, Robert Louis Stevenson, and Charles Dickens were moldy and their gilt lettering faded. Atop the bookcase was a fully mounted, exceedingly dusty bald eagle whose once fierce golden eyes were nearly opaque as a result of a thick coating of old tobacco smoke. The television was a sixties-vintage Zenith in a walnut console with rabbit ears that pointed disconsolately blankly at the overstuffed Duncan Phyfe sofa upholstered in alternating red-and-white striped cotton. An unwashed, superannuated black Labrador lay sound asleep on an equally filthy, once red comforter.

Ted Sanders, dressed in his father's elegant dressing gown, sat facing Pastor Peter who was wearing his ecclesiastical collar, shirt, and coat. A clean empty water glass stood on a side table next to Ted and another half full was beside the pastor. Both men had large, black-leather Bibles on their laps opened to the Book of Ecclesiastes. Pastor Peter nodded approvingly and spoke.

"The heart of the wise is in the house of morning, but Ted remember the prophet also speaks of a time to heal."

Ted nodded.

"Amen to that Reverend. But, God forgive me, even with the comfort of the Good Book, I still find it harder and harder to get up in the morning."

"It's normal to feel depressed since your wife passed away. Everyone who loses a loved one goes through that. You miss her."

Ted looked him directly in the eye.

"Pastor, you're wrong. I miss her like I miss a bad charley horse. Laura spent thirty years dragging and ragging me down. There used to be a thousand acres around this house planted in fine tobacco. Now Sanders Plantation has less than a hundred, most of it is milkweed, thistle, and dust."

Trying to recover from his gaffe Pastor Peter replied brightly.

"You still have a lovely daughter."

Ted's face flushed and his hands clenched in anger.

"Lovely but not loving. She holds me responsible for her mother's death."

"But your wife died from congestive heart failure."

"Facts don't matter to Stephanie. She blames me. She blames me for everything bad that ever happened to her and her mother and for every animal that ever met a bad end. She thinks I'm Satan incarnate or something like that."

Ted was on the verge of flying into a rage. He continued in a voice that was almost hysterical.

"She should be a comfort to me in my old age. She should have made the Sanders name proud, carrying it on by giving me a grandson with a husband of family, integrity, and character. Instead all she's given me is a bastard granddaughter and she won't even tell me who the bastard's father is."

At this jeremiad, Pastor Peter nervously cleared his throat. Ted leaned in close to him and locked eyes.

"Reverend, you're the only man in this godforsaken county that understands the Bible and what it really means to be a Christian. I swear to you if I ever find the man who raped my daughter I'll kill him if it's my last act on earth."

Pastor Peter paled as the blood drained from his face, which fortunately Ted was too distraught to notice.

"Ted, as your minister let me assure you the Lord would have you feel differently about Stephanie."

He used her name hoping that by naming her Ted might soften his attitude and his rhetoric. He added,

"Why would you say she was raped?"

"Is there really any difference between raping a girl and having sex with a Christian woman out of wedlock?"

Pastor Peter was too afraid of Ted to roll his eyes heavenward at what Peter believed as an absurd misinterpretation of various scriptural admonitions though Ted might have been espousing a better conception of the Hebrew scriptural attitude toward premarital coitus than he realized.

"God grant you peace, Ted."

Pastor Peter stood and Ted stood as well.

"Please forgive me Reverend if I've offended you but a man's got to have values."

Pastor Peter stepped carefully over the recumbent, unconscious Labrador on his way out of the study leaving Ted to address the closing door.

"A life without values is a life without value."

Pastor Peter walked to his SUV and drove slowly away. As he passed Stevie's trailer he saw Gigi who began to dance up and down and wave excitedly. Stevie emerged and Peter rolled down his window. With a gesture that clearly indicated he could not stop, he waved goodbye. Stevie heard Ted's tractor and after a moment Ted approached riding on the old John Deere and pointedly ignoring both his daughter and granddaughter as he passed them. As she gestured to Gigi, the little girl joined her and the two of them entered the trailer. Ted craned his head around and watched them as the Airstream door closed.

As Pastor Peter exited the Sanders's driveway and was about to turn right, his SUV was almost T-boned by an old Ford wrecker with a loud muffler that raced by at more than sixty miles an hour.

"What the f . . . ?"

He bit off the expletive and stamped the accelerator pedal to catch the truck and with every intention of giving them hell. As he neared the wrecker he saw a young man in a ball cap glancing through the rear window laughing. The bumper sticker read "H&B Wrecking, Zion." He knew enough of these notorious, local miscreants to quickly decide that discretion was the better part of valor. He slowed then made a U-turn and headed in the opposite direction.

CHAPTER 7

Inside a "Clean Room"

Atop the plastic walnut-veneered dresser stood several black, metal frame photographs bought at a Walmart. In one, two uniformed law enforcement officers, a deputy sheriff and the other a New Orleans policeman, Luke and Daniel Olsen respectively, smiled winningly into the camera. Daniel's clothes were strewn about and an empty bottle of Popov vodka on the dresser made the room look untidy and slipshod. Daniel lay in his underwear on the unmade bed staring at the dingy, white painted cottage ceiling. He heard a rather sharp knock on the door.

"Who is it?"

"Your father."

Daniel got up, still in his underwear, opened the door with a heavy sigh and sat down in the lone armchair, draped with his police uniform. Sheriff Olsen in full uniform looked at the Popov bottle with upper lip curled in distaste, then at Daniel who fastened a bath towel around his waist. The sheriff looked at his oversize stainless steel wristwatch.

"It's nearly eleven in the morning."

Daniel stared at the red LED numbers on the clock radio.

"So it is."

"You never told me your plans."

"I really don't have any."

"Look, Daniel. I'm getting on with it and so should you."

"Uh huh. That's easy for you to say."

The sheriff was hurt, which was neither easy nor often. Daniel could not remember the last time he had really hurt his rock of a father and this added to a crushing burden of shame and guilt. The sheriff said quietly:

"No, not really."

Daniel looked his father squarely in the eyes.

"I skipped town with Luke's wife. Dad. These things don't just happen."

"Okay. You're right. You're an irresponsible, worthless drunk and a really shitty brother, not to mention a world-class disappointment of a son. There! Does that make you happy? You should never have left town. Luke missed you a thousand times more than he missed that rotten traitorous bitch of a wife of his who ran off with you. He loved you till the day he died."

Sheriff Olsen continued.

"So you're headed back to New Orleans? Back to the witch?"

"No. She left me two years ago. Thought maybe I'd move on. Cincinnati, Chicago maybe, I don't know really."

"Run away. That's always been your answer hasn't it?"

"I suppose it has."

"Well this time maybe just maybe you could show some guts and do the right thing for once. Luke left me shorthanded."

"I appreciate the offer but I think I'll be moving on."

The sheriff looked utterly disgusted. Daniel hesitated for a long moment reconsidering the possibility, seeing it as one way to atone for what he had done to Luke and his father.

"All right I'll think about it."

"You do that."

Pastor Peter recovered from his near-death experience with the H&B tow truck by riding his chestnut Tennessee walking horse, Traveler. He usually rode in an arena near his church. The weather was sufficiently warm for comfort and, in fact, his head was sweating slightly in the black felt hard hat he favored. As he trotted he noticed Traveler was gaiting just slightly off his usual smooth stride and seemed to be favoring his right rear leg. He dismounted then lifted the rear leg repeatedly, massaging the hock as he did. A very well mannered horse, Traveler not only did not mind the pastor's ministrations, but also he seemed to appreciate them. Now, sweating with the effort, Pastor Peter released the leg and led his horse out of the arena.

Stevie had set up her small, colorful canvas tent by the roadside in a flat, not too dusty turnout. On each side of the road, a white board sign with black lettering read: "CLINIC TODAY 11–2." Another in psychedelic colors with well-drawn, black letter calligraphy read, "Animal Healing Here." Inside the tent Stevie sat on a canvas folding chair behind a red vinyl-topped, folding, black metal bridge table and a green medical chest. Gigi was playing with a troop of plastic toy animals of various species. A pretty young woman named Renee dressed in torn blue jeans and a white T-shirt devoid of logos entered with a very large dog, definitely part English mastiff, mixed with several others, possibly Rottweiler. The dog was imposing and looked anything but happy.

Renee said tearfully:

"Wolfy just started snapping at me this morning. It scared me. He's never done that before."

Stevie laid her hands on the beast stroking his sides and then his legs. She looked at his eyes and fearlessly opened his huge mouth revealing slightly yellowed and carious fangs.

"Honestly he's in fairly good health for a what is he now? Ten?"

"He's almost eleven."

"Well now that he's an elderly gentleman, it takes him more time to wake up. Don't rush in on him. Let him know you're coming."

"Anything else? He really frightened me."

Wolfy gazed at Stevie affectionately and she scratched him behind the ear eliciting a deep-throated contented groan.

"Well I get the feeling Wolfy would like some nice new tennis balls; the bright yellow ones that are easy for him to see and chase."

"My boyfriend wants me to get rid of him. Says he gets in the way of the two of us."

"Wolfy will be there for you long after your boyfriend's history. I'd ditch him and keep the dog."

Renee grinned and took a twenty from her purse and handed it to Stevie just as Pastor Peter pulled up. Renee and Wolfy walked to her car. Stevie smiled warmly as Pastor Peter exited his SUV and walked up.

"Hey you," said Stevie. "What a pleasant surprise."

"I hope you're not too busy for me."

He kissed her affectionately on the right cheek.

"I've been having trouble with Traveler. We tried trotting earlier this afternoon but he wasn't gaiting well."

"It's probably that hip joint again."

"I massaged his leg and he liked it but it didn't help. If it would just lock up tight I could have the vet blister him."

Stevie said sharply:

"And why the hell would you do a dumb thing like that? The vet sent you to me in the first place."

"How could I ever forget?"

"You drove off the farm this morning like you'd seen the devil himself. You could have stopped for a coffee."

"That might have been unwise after the conversation I had with your father."

Stevie began straightening out her instruments and medicaments.

"I take it he still hates me."

"Actually he maintains it's you who hates him. You two really should try to communicate, if not for yourself, then for Gigi's sake, for all three of your sakes."

Stevie replied, long-standing frustration evident in her tone.

"Peter, I love that you're kind to him. But you shouldn't meddle in things you don't understand. You simply weren't around when things got really bad between us. And it seems like they've only gotten worse in the last couple of years."

Gigi ran up and Pastor Peter lifted her up while continuing the conversation.

"I'd be a poor minister if I didn't at least try to reconcile the two of you. Remember, my father was his pastor. They had a trust that I have a responsibility to continue."

"Why is this so important to you all of a sudden?"

At that moment, a white Ford F-150 drove up with a large and majestically horned billy goat standing in the bed.

"I'll be done here soon. I can see you and Traveler later this afternoon."

Pastor Peter nodded his assent as a weathered, fifty-year-old white man in soiled blue overalls led his large billy goat tied on a thick hemp rope past him. The man nodded to the pastor.

"You ain't gonna believe what he did to me this morning!"

Stevie looked dubiously at the large and obviously agitated goat. She looked at the owner then pulled up a rough hewn, oak tripod stool and studied the goat's backside.

"What exactly did he do?"

"He up and butted me and while I was down I think he was trying to, well you know."

"Mount you?"

The man flushed.

Just as Stevie was going to reply and Pastor Peter's SUV was disappearing, the H&B tow truck with Hank and Bill slowed as it came near to the tent. Hank was in the driver's seat and Bill was chewing on a thoroughly spit-soaked Swisher Sweet cigar.

Seeing Stevie's signs he said to Bill:

"Look! There's that crazy, animal-loving freak again. She always hangs around here."

Bill shifted the Swisher from the right side of his mouth to the left.

"Uh-huh. Healer my ass! She's a bitch witch."

As the truck slowly rumbled by Bill gave Stevie a menacing glance and an upraised middle finger, which was yellowed with tobacco and featured a long, filthy and chipped nail.

Stevie looked up from the goat and returned Bill's look with an angelic smile and forked her index and middle finger in the peace sign. Hank gunned the engine enveloping Stevie in a diffuse cloud of exhaust smoke. The goat's owner commented dryly:

"For two guys who are supposed to know about trucks, theirs ain't in good shape. Burning oil. Probably needs new head gaskets."

Stevie nodded and then turned her attention to the goat putting both hands on the long, curving etiolated horns and looked into its limpid blue right eye.

Daniel Olsen was wide awake in his darkened room. All the curtains were drawn so that virtually no light entered through the edges. He switched on the nightstand light and rubbed his eyes against the glare. Having finished this morning ritual he opened them and looked at the photograph of him and Luke. He sat for a long moment then quickly pulled on his blue jeans and buttoned his light gray flannel shirt, donned his Maui Jim style reflective sunglasses, and opening the door walked out into the afternoon glare.

A late model red Dodge Ram pick-up truck was parked in a backfield on Sanders Plantation, gate down with boxes of Winchester ammunition on top.

Sheriff Olsen squeezed the trigger of a deluxe Winchester takedown 1894 rifle and one hundred yards down range a plastic gallon jug filled with water exploded. He smiled and handed the Winchester to Ted.

"Nice old weapon. Must be worth quite a bit of money."

Ted worked the lever chambering another round.

"Belonged to my father. Used it to go hunting with your old man."

Ted aimed and fired at the remnants of the jug hitting the handle section sending it a foot in the air.

Sheriff Olsen said, "Nice shot. That must have been about forty years ago."

"Closer to fifty. After the Second War."

"Got to get back to town, Ted. See you out here same time next Tuesday?"

Ted nodded.

"Your father was a good man, Robert. Coming from a good family's everything."

Ted raised the rifle, aimed, and fired exploding another water-filled plastic jug. Sheriff Olsen walked to his truck.

Daniel parked his truck on the grassy lane, which encircled the Zion Baptist Church cemetery. He exited then walked quickly to the freshly turned earth of Luke's grave. He knelt on the margin then removed his well-worn, leather police badge case from his hip pocket. He carefully unpinned the shield and as he held it in his left hand out at arm's length contemplating it, a beam of sunlight struck the silver star and crescent badge of the New Orleans Police Department. He scooped a deep hole into the loose earth of the grave near the simple, white marble headstone. He placed the badge in the hole and carefully filled it with earth then gently tamped it down.

CHAPTER 8

Horsing Around

Pastor Peter had parked his white-and-gray, bumper-pull Solemate horse trailer alongside the arena he rented. Inside the pipe-rail-fenced arena Stevie was gently coaxing Traveler on a lead rope to a slow trot. Pastor Peter looked on somewhat anxiously. Stevie carefully studied the horse's gait, focusing on the hindquarters. She halted him, walked up and began vigorously massaging the right rear leg, first the thigh and then down to the stifle.

Pastor Peter asked, "What do you think?"

"We were right. It's that hip again. Hold him."

Stevie opened her medicament chest and removed a foul-smelling concoction of her own make from an amber glass jar. Taking a scoop with her right hand she worked the mixture into the hip. She followed this up with a small amount of a less odoriferous white ointment. After these ministrations she took a small, white aluminum tube laser from her jeans and began moving it up and down the affected area.

Pastor Peter smiled broadly.

"I remember that day six years ago when I first met you with your herbal remedies and the little magic torch."

Stevie continued with the laser.

"Mm. Hm. And I recall you caused quite a stir when you returned from Yale Divinity School."

"I had to come back. Dad was ready to retire and move to Florida. Besides I wanted to bring the Zion Baptist community into the twenty-first century."

"I still can't believe my father accepted you like he did. He's so Old Testament."

Stevie continued the laser treatment.

"Um . . . Honey, we really need to speak seriously."

Stevie paused and looked up.

"Is that why you got me down here? This is not the right time."

"I'm sorry. It's just that when you're close to me like this it's not easy. I want us to be like we used to be. Like we're meant to be."

"But it's nothing like it used to be. My whole life's changed now that Gigi's here. And you couldn't understand that until you've lived it. You're being unfair."

"But you think it's fair that Gabriella doesn't know I'm her father?"

"We agreed we'd wait."

"No. You said we had to wait. You needed time to adjust. Well, time's growing short."

Stevie stopped and her tone was flat, almost menacing.

"Are you threatening me?"

"No. God clearly states, 'If a man entice a maid that is not betrothed, he shall surely endow her to be his wife.' Exodus: 4:13."

Stevie ignored this and began to pick up her instruments.

"My father always quoted scripture like that. That was usually just before he hit my mother."

Pastor Peter gently grasped her shoulder.

"Stevie. You and your father simply must reconcile. Without genuine forgiveness neither of you can possibly heal."

Stevie said, the heat in her voice obvious and compelling,

"No way! He needs to apologize for slowly killing my mother and ruining our lives. What does any of that have to do with you and me anyway? We were talking about us, right?"

"I think the two are linked."

"You're a minister not my therapist."

"Listen Stevie, he's a tired, embittered, lonely old man and when he dies you'll be sorry."

"All right. I'll make you a deal. If you stop pressuring me I'll think about it. Okay?"

CHAPTER 9

George at Home

George Jackson was in his modest but immaculate kitchen chopping carrots on an ancient, maple butcher block. He was looking at the slave shack in the distance, his hands dexterously handling the razor-sharp knife chopping rhythmically while Delta blues played softly on the small, black Sony clock radio. Gigi Sanders appeared suddenly behind him, her pretty face painted in an amateurish imitation of a tiger complete with stripes. She held an old and well-worn brass thimble. George ceased chopping and smiled. Gigi held it out to give him a better look not that he needed it.

"Grandpa George, what's this?"

"That used to belong to your Auntie Faith, my better half, Gigi girl."

"What's it for?"

"It's her old thimble."

George took the thimble and placed it on his weathered right thumb.

"See you put it on your thumb like this. That was you don't stick yourself while you're sewing. Auntie Faith used it to make shirts, sweaters, and things to keep you warm."

Gigi pulled up an old shawl, which had been carefully draped over a folded wheelchair leaning against the wall. She artfully draped the shawl around her shoulders though it was long and a considerable length of it was on the wood floor.

"You mean like this""

"Yes, little one. Just like that."

CHAPTER 10

Back in Harness

The Zion sheriff's office was a rather informal edifice. The exterior was red brick with aluminum windows except for the windowless back, which housed two holding cells. No one was ever jailed for more than a day or two as inmates were swiftly transported to the less luxurious county jail. The interior consisted of a waist-high, oak kiosk with the usual aluminum-banded, gray Formica office desks behind which sat on an institutional, variegated linoleum floor. There were only four desks topped with Dell computers. In one corner stood a Universal Police Weapons cabinet with three Colt M-16 automatic rifles and three parkerized Ithaca Model 37 12-gauge riot shotguns, not that any deputy had used one of the rifles for anything other than an afternoon's target shooting. The dramatic rise in the price of ammunition had made this a rare event in recent years.

Daniel rather timidly pushed open the heavy glass-and-aluminum door with the black block print lettering spelling out "Zion Sheriff's Office." His father was sitting at his desk with the wood-and-brass triangular desk sign that said "Sheriff." Daniel spoke in a tone reflecting a confidence he did not really feel.

"Hey!"

Sheriff Olsen looked up with a wry grin.

"You made it."

Daniel looked around registering the desks, computers, and the weapons cabinet.

"Everything looks about the same. Well almost everything."

Daniel's gaze fixed on a very attractive, statuesque, African American woman in her late twenties with coffee-colored skin and regular features with a short but stylish Afro, dressed in a thin khaki blouse and dangerously short matching khaki shorts. She was lifting a glazed donut from a bag of Krispy Kremes. Noticing his son staring fixedly at his secretary, the sheriff coughed.

"Daniel, this is Cheryl Johnson. She tries to make herself useful around here."

Cheryl was checking out Daniel and liked what she saw.

"Hey," she said.

"Hey yourself."

The sheriff poured Daniel a coffee from the glass Bunn carafe and walked to a wall closet. Daniel sipped his coffee and watched as Cheryl bit off a large section of the glazed donut and some crystals adhered to the fine hair on her upper lip. Daniel thought he would give quite a lot to lick off the sugar crystals. Sheriff Olsen withdrew a freshly pressed Zion deputy's uniform and held it out to his son.

"I think this should fit you."

Cheryl smiled and looked at Daniel.

"I hope it does too."

There was an implication in her silky voice that she was really hoping the uniform fitted in more ways than one. Noticing there was evidently chemistry between the two younger people he said a bit sharply to Cheryl:

"Don't you have something better to do?"

Daniel took the uniform and held it to his chest, sizing it.

"Daniel. One thing. You'd better not be doing this as a favor to me."

Daniel paused a moment and replied with sincerity:

"No. It's an honor to wear it. Now, if you'll excuse me I'm going to change."

Before he left for the bathroom he glanced back as Cheryl licked the sugar off her upper lip. The sheriff saw him and flashed him a disapproving look.

"What are you looking at, son?"

"Nothing."

Daniel walked in the direction of the bathroom holding the uniform on its hanger. The sheriff nodded and somewhat agitated spilled some of his coffee on the linoleum.

"Shit."

He looked at Cheryl who could not suppress a grin.

"Clean that up, will you?"

Cheryl was still smiling as the sheriff walked out the door leaving her and Daniel in charge. As he left he mumbled to himself.

"Might not be such a bad thing after all."

Ted Sanders was examining his antique firearms collection inherited from his Confederate ancestors and relatives late into the night. He waxed them with care and contemplated each one as if they were pets, which in a sense they were. He mumbled to himself as if speaking to the gun: "What

do you want from me?" He picked up a LeMat revolver, stared at it then left the great room carrying the revolver. Entering the master bedroom Ted sat heavily in one of the two overstuffed, faded, red-velvet covered, mahogany-framed easy chairs with lion's paw armrests, the LeMat across his lap. He stared at a quite well-rendered portrait of his wife painted shortly after their wedding as a gift from her parents. The artist was a locally famous Charleston portrait painter and he had succeeded in capturing Laura Sanders's subtle beauty, one mixed with an intelligence that was particularly evident in the eyes. The painting was framed in an elaborate Louis XV-style gilt frame. After a long moment, his overtired eyes were moist and he said clearly to his wife's image:

"Sorry. I'm so sorry, my love."

CHAPTER 11

Hunter's Bar

Hunter's Bar was not named because of its association with hunters, though its honey-colored, varnished, knotty-pine walls were festooned with glassy-eyed, dead deer head mounts, shelves featuring full-mount raccoons, squirrels, and various game birds. On the mahogany bar was an oversized glass jar with a screw top and a decal of the NRA reading, "Donations" in addition to a stand-up cardboard sign reading, "Hunting and Fishing Licenses Sold Here." The eponymous owner, Duncan Hunter, was an affable fifty year old with a thick mop of graying dark hair, a face with pleasantly regular features, and a fit five-foot-eleven body. Duncan habitually dressed in fresh, dry-cleaned khakis. Daniel and the sheriff were sitting at one of the low wood tables with a thick epoxy coating. The sheriff was enjoying a quiet, frosty, thick-faceted glass mug of draft Stella Artois, which Duncan had recently introduced to the Zion bar scene not

that there was any scene at all apart from Hunter's, while Daniel sipped a coffee in a thick china cup.

An attractive blond in her late thirties with long, well-kempt hair and a face that required no makeup was sitting on a red leatherette stool nursing a martini at the bar, rather obviously checking out Daniel. Duncan eyed her narrowly, obviously not a regular, as he took the sheriff's empty mug.

"Another round for Zion's finest?"

The sheriff replied,

"No thanks, Duncan, I'm good."

Daniel winked at Duncan,

"I can handle another cup of coffee."

Daniel swiveled his head and looked at the blond who had finished her martini and was now drinking a bottle of Miller Lite. He turned back to the sheriff.

"Think I'll hang out here for a while, Dad."

The sheriff stood up and tossed a twenty on the table.

"You take care of yourself."

"Count on it."

The sheriff paused for a moment and looked searchingly at his only surviving child.

"See you bright and early."

Daniel nodded his assent as Sheriff Olsen walked out of the bar. He pushed back his chair and joined the blond at the bar. Duncan set another martini in front of the woman and brought Daniel a fresh cup of coffee. Daniel looked at Duncan.

"Duncan, put this young lady's drink on my tab and why don't we change the coffee to something cold."

Knowing the Olsen brothers penchant for alcohol only too well, Duncan looked at him hard.

"You sure?"

"I'm sure."

The following morning Stevie was in her trailer looking in the mirror and noticing the almost imperceptible lines at the corners of her wide mouth and full lips. She was frowning when her landline rang.

"Stevie Sanders?"

"Yes. Yes! I'm getting ready to go now. I will be there in twenty minutes. Yes, I know it's an emergency."

She hung up and swiftly pulled on a pair of supple, black leather boots.

Zeke was putting the finishing polish on the Gorham silver coffee service on the white damask linen tablecloth. Satisfied, he disappeared into the Abbott mansion walking past the gleaming black Lincoln Town Car.

At the Sanders mansion Ted was in the process of raising his faded and tattered Confederate flag as he did every morning in fair weather. Stevie walked past her truck, down the driveway toward the main house.

CHAPTER 12

Mourning Muffy

Zeke reappeared with a folded American flag followed by Lucille Abbott dressed in a sleeve wrap, white Halston jump suit with tie waist.

"One lump or two today, ma'am?"

Lucille's carefully applied mascara was running, endangering the pristine whiteness of her suit. Her eyes were puffy from weeping.

"One, please. Or perhaps I could use two today. It's all so sad Zeke, all so sad."

"We all have to meet our Maker sometime, Miss Abbott."

Lucille sighed again, more deeply this time.

"I should have taken Muffy to the Sanders girl. My veterinarian is a useless imbecile."

"Begging your pardon, ma'am, but she's gone to a better place where she can run and play."

Lucille sniffed and removed an embroidered hanky from the pocket of her morning suit.

"I suppose you are right. She wasn't walking too well toward the end."

Zeke nodded and attached the flag to its rope. He untied the cord and prepared to raise it when Lucille called to him.

"Half-staff if you please, Zeke. For the next seven days."

Zeke rolled his eyes heavenward and muttered softly under his breath so Lucille would not hear it.

"People 'round here must think we're crazy."

With that said he raised the flag half way and tied the cord around the aluminum fitting.

Ted was seated on his John Deere, working the scoop up and down checking the hydraulics, which either had a leak or air in the lines. As Stevie approached he left off his testing and shut off the motor. His face, habitually dark with a lifetime of dissatisfaction, unrealized hopes, and disgust with contemporary American life in general, darkened further. Stevie cleared her throat and said in a friendly tone.

"Good morning."

Ted climbed down off the tractor. He sneered sarcastically.

"My daughter hasn't spoken to me in months and that's all she has to say to her father—'Good morning'?

"I didn't come here to fight. I'd like to make my peace with you. Once and for all."

"You spend more time tending to your animals than you do to your own blood."

"That's 'cause some people spend so much time killing them."

"But now they that are younger than I, have me in derision. They abhor me, they flee far from me, and spare not to spit in my face."

"When are you going to stop using scripture as a weapon?"

"When you get right with the Lord. When are you going to understand what it means to be an unmarried woman with a child? You're a disgrace to the Sanders, to all women for that matter."

Stevie shook her head slowly.

"I'm sorry about many things but not about Gigi. I love her more than all the world and if you gave her a chance you would too."

Ted snarled.

"Just tell me her father's name."

Stevie replied softly, the regret evident in her voice.

"I see you haven't changed. Well maybe you have, you've gotten worse."

Ted said harshly, his pent-up frustration mixing with anger.

"Don't you dare talk to your father that way!"

"I've waited and waited for you to forgive me, so that maybe we could forgive each other. But I'm not waiting any longer. We're leaving. Me and Gigi."

Ted scoffed derisively.

"You can't go. Who would want you anyway?"

"Well. I'll move in with George. George Jackson. He'll be more than happy to take us in."

Ted stepped toward Stevie red faced and furious.

"That's insane! Jackson's used to be sharecroppers, field hands, our slaves. You can't do this to me!"

"That's the most disgusting thing I've ever heard. I go where I'm wanted and so does Gigi."

Stevie looked around the plantation.

"And we're not wanted here."

Ted's voice was icy.

"Stephanie. I'm warning you. Don't do this to me. Don't do this to the Sanders family."

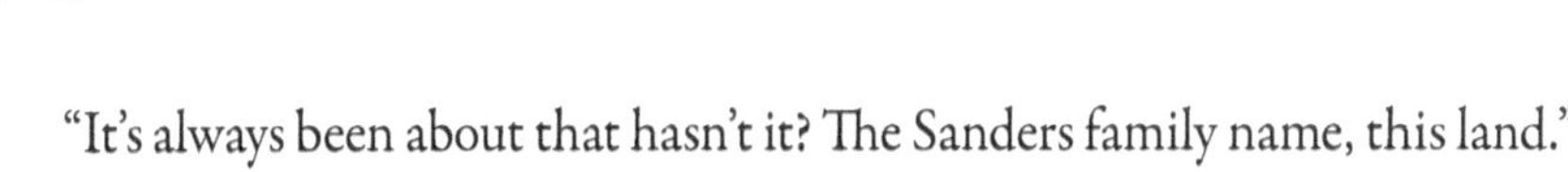

"It's always been about that hasn't it? The Sanders family name, this land."

Here she pointed at the Stars and Bars.

"That flag, all your guns."

Ted sagged slightly and sat down on the tractor's scoop. He said in a tired voice, incredulous at his daughter's rejection of all he held dear.

"They're our family's heritage. Our sacred treasured relics. Relics of our gallant resistance to the War of Northern Aggression."

"Take a look around, Dad. The way you talk. The way you think. The only real relic around here is you."

Stevie turned and walked away swiftly holding back tears. Ted stared after her. He looked up to the Confederate banner for reassurance.

He called after her retreating figure.

"Remember I warned you . . . I wash my hands of the consequences and you."

Stevie ran the final few yards to her trailer. Her heart was racing and on entering she grabbed an old American Tourister red suitcase and began mindlessly packing her few valuables and some clothes. She flipped open a thin Yellow Pages and scanned the entries under "Trailer Movers/Wrecking Service." A large, black ceramic horse was standing on a table with the telephone book and when she moved the book it fell and shattered on the floor. Stevie burst into tears but quickly regained her equanimity as one of her mixed-breed, shaggy rescue dogs looked up at her puzzled to see his master in such an agitated state.

"Come here, Alvie, mama's okay."

Alvie wagged his stumpy tail and leapt into her arms. Stevie rubbed the soft fur on Alvie's ears.

"Mama's going to be just fine . . ."

CHAPTER 13

Moving On

George Jackson and Gigi were trimming grass and pulling weeds around the myriad miniature white crosses on and among the far more venerable and aging human graves with their simple marble headstones. George was using a gasoline-powered trimmer with a nylon cord while Gigi was pulling up the wild onions and smelling both the uprooted onions and her hands, reveling in the pungent aroma. The low white picket border fences had significant gaps as a result of the frequent reuse of the stakes for crosses. As George lifted the trimmer he experienced a momentary shortness of breath. He laid down the trimmer and felt his chest. Gigi saw Stevie's truck approach, dropped a particularly luxuriant clump of onions and ran to the truck. Stevie opened the driver's door and stepped out. Her normally well-groomed long hair was tangled and her face was tear-stained. George left off palpating his left breast.

"What is it, girl?"

Stevie swept Gigi up in her arms then said breathlessly:

"I just had it out with my father once and for all. I told him we were packing up for good."

"The poor man, I can't help but feel sorry for him."

Stevie said incredulously:

"What is this? Feel sorry for Ted Day? The man hates your guts. You might live in that nice little house on the hill, but that slave shack in the middle of Little Souls is where my father thinks you belong and every one of your ancestors that ever lived."

George's tone acknowledged the justice of Stevie's words. He nodded.

"You're right. It's just I know how hard it is to lose a wife and go on living."

"But you loved your wife. He despised my mother almost every day of her life."

"Are you sure? After all he never remarried when he had the chance."

George sat down on the grass and locked his eyes on Stevie's for a moment then he switched to something going on behind her. A gleaming black Lincoln Town car pulled up and off the gravel onto the grass. The driver rolled down the window. George and the unknown driver of the Town Car conversed out of Stevie's earshot. Then the shining black Lincoln pulled away at a funeral pace. Stevie thought she recognized the car.

"Was that Lucille Abbott's car?" George walked back to her and nodded, his face creased in a thin smile.

"She lost her kitty."

"Wants to bury it here?"

"Richest lady in Zion wants nothing but the best for her departed "Muffy."

George withdrew his old, battered, silver hunting case railroad watch, an inheritance from his father and checked the time.

"Don't tell me she wants it this afternoon."

George nodded, grinning broadly this time.

"I'm a pallbearer. And not a day too soon."

"You behind in your mortgage again?"

George nodded grimly and nodded.

"Social Security and all don't cover the needs of life out here."

"Well you heard me. We're moving in. I'll pay you rent."

"With what? We're both one-step ahead of the bill collector. When are you coming over?"

Stevie said mischievously:

"Better a step ahead than behind. I told Ted we'd be gone by morning. Tow truck's coming over at the end of the day."

George looked at the western sky.

"Then we have one whole lot of work to do today."

Stevie grinned broadly and kissed George firmly on his right cheek as Gigi bearhugged his left leg.

CHAPTER 14

Burying Muffy

When Stevie arrived at Little Souls later that day dressed in a dark blue Marshalls shirt and skirt, which she hoped appeared sufficiently reverent for the occasion, George was already waiting, having donned his one black suit inherited from his father. A rather pretty young woman with waist-length blond hair whom Stevie did not recognize was playing "Now We Gather at the River" on a fairly large, gilt wood harp. George looked at his pocket watch. Lucille Abbott's gleaming black Lincoln approached at a funeral pace then stopped near the freshly dug grave. The trunk was opened from the inside revealing a richly appointed, miniature, black ebonized casket with gilt bronze handles and a brilliant brass nameplate finely engraved reading, "MUFFY."

Dressed in a stylish black Armani tuxedo complete with black tie, Ezekiel opened the passenger door for Lucille Abbott, who was attired

in a Valentino jet black, lace-mourning dress. George approached and he and Zeke as if by previous agreement each grasped a handle of the coffin as Stevie and Gigi stood silently and impassively as the blond harpist played the funeral march from Chopin's piano sonata number 2. Lucille stood ramrod straight and stone faced next to Stevie. Ezekiel was fidgeting in a vain attempt to repress a smirk so he turned away. Lucille's gaze remained fixed on the new earth mounded beside the grave. Zeke and George used the thick, braided, gold velvet ropes to lower the casket into the grave. Stevie pressed Lucille's soft, damp right hand as the final harp string sounded the end of the march. Lucille turned to her as George and Zeke filled in the grave. Lucille's voice trembled with emotion.

"Oh, Stevie, it's all too beautiful, a truly perfect service. I just know Muffy will be happy here."

Stevie touched Lucille's shoulder as tears streamed down Mrs. Abbott's face.

"I'm sure Muffy's in heaven, looking down and smiling."

Lucille left off weeping and said somewhat doubtfully:

"Are you certain? There were those mice and several cute little toads."

Lucille hesitated then continued.

"And she did torture those three baby bunny rabbits to death. Maybe she went to . . ."

"Mrs. Abbott, animals obey the nature God gives them. They don't have a choice. People do"

Lucille perseverated about the baby rabbits.

"Those poor little bunnies. When she was through they were nothing more than bloody tufts of fur."

Stevie was growing increasingly annoyed by what she saw as a ludicrously ostentatious funeral for a housecat. She had seen hundreds of what she regarded as little souls interred with dignified simplicity. She thought

Muffy's casket probably cost considerably more than her mother's or Mr. Abbott's for that matter.

"Lucille, I already told you that's her nature. That's her job."

Lucille bridled at this condemning her just buried cat. She said in an accusatory tone as if Stevie were an uneducated country bumpkin:

"Young lady, perhaps you're too young to recall, but that's exactly what all those Nazis said after World War Two, 'We were only following orders.'"

Coming after all her efforts to console the bereaved feline owner, compounded by the absurd spectacle of black suited and tuxedoed pallbearers, a pretty, talented harpist, and a coffin that cost several thousand dollars proved too much for Stevie. She exploded.

"Fine! Have it your way. Muffy is paying for her crimes. She's roasting in Satan's fiery furnace even as we speak. Is that what you want to hear? And what the hell do the Nazis have to do with your cat Muffy? How can you even compare the two?"

Lucille was stunned. She replied in a subdued voice:

"I'm sorry. It's just that I live alone. Since Mr. Abbott passed away Muffy has been my only companion in that great big house. Everything has been very confusing."

Stevie experienced a sharp pang thinking of when she lost her mother.

"I'm sorry I lost my temper."

Stevie reached out to hug Lucille but the older woman pulled away and smoothed her dress. George signaled to the harpist who stopped playing.

Lucille composed herself and her thoughts returned to what she saw as a fitting tribute to Muffy, all thoughts of butchered bunnies vanished.

"Such a moving service. Muffy's in heaven now."

Stevie nodded. Lucille continued.

"I'm sure God won't punish her. After all He made her."

"That's exactly how I see it."

Stevie and George looked at each other while Lucille motioned to Zeke.

"Ezekiel, my checkbook, please."

He handed her a gilt-stamped, beige leather checkbook.

"My pen, please."

Zeke withdrew a gold Montblanc Petite Prince fountain pen and handed it to Lucille.

She wrote out a check and signed with a flourish, handing the three items to Zeke who pocketed two and passed the check to Stevie who accepted it gracefully.

"Ezekiel, I'll be going home now."

"Yes ma'am. I'll take you to the car."

The financial formalities concluded, Lucille turned away from Stevie and George without a backward glance. Zeke held open the passenger door for Lucille and nodded to George who nodded back. Still holding the check in her right hand Stevie decided to look at it and her eyes widened. She showed it to George who whistled softly at the amount. Stevie paid the harpist with twenty-dollar bills and thanked her. Everyone watched as the shining black car drove away slowly, all except for Gigi who was digging with both her hands in the newly turned earth mound covering Muffy's grave.

CHAPTER 15

Transitions

That afternoon after Muffy's funeral, Ted Sanders was carefully but somewhat ineptly writing an address with a black Sharpie on a long rectangular pine crate. The address read "Lewis & Grant Auctions, 111 Beech Street, Newport, Kentucky." Completing this task, he looked at a folded letter and ciphering the zip code, added it. He startled at the sound of a large truck outside on the gravel.

Stevie and George were packing the last of her belongings into U-Haul cardboard boxes when a large wrecking truck pulled up. Stevie was shocked to see the logo on the truck door. Inside the cab Hank and Bill were as shocked as Stevie. Hank spoke to Bill.

"Holy shit."

Bill was incredulous.

"Didn't you know who was calling us?"

They looked at each other with furrowed brows. Hank spoke first.

"We need the cash, Bill. Just don't tell anyone we were here."

George looked quizzically at Stevie. He sensed the wrecking truck was trouble. Hank and Bill got out of the truck; their muscular, tattooed upper arms peeked out of their black H&B T-shirts.

"I take it you know these boys."

Stevie had a metallic taste in her throat.

"Well, sort of."

No one looked pleased with the situation. Ted observed the action from a distance as Hank backed up the H&B wrecker to hook up Stevie's trailer. His face was flushed with anger.

"That seals it," he said muttering ominously to himself.

Daniel's modest room was bathed in candlelight. Spa music floated softly out of the clock radio. A Zion County deputy sheriff's badge glowed on the dresser together with his service automatic pistol. He was naked and perspiring as he rolled off Cheryl and lay on his back exhausted and breathing heavily. After a few moments he rolled off the bed, stood and began to dress. Cheryl said inquiringly:

"Want me to go?"

"Well, you know I got things to do . . ."

After putting on his uniform pants he leaned down over the bed and kissed her gently on her full lips.

"You know. You're beautiful."

Cheryl laughed.

"Right. Not beautiful enough to keep me here longer."

He buttoned his uniform shirt.

"Hey. It ain't like that."

"It's all right. I understand."

Cheryl turned over, left the bed, and began to dress.

George Jackson left his home with a well-used mattock over his right shoulder. Stevie's trailer stood on the left side of the house a few feet from the outside wall. George walked through the field of miniature white crosses and came to a stop next to a new, obviously full, white plastic trash bag, which rested on the grass. He swung the mattock and it bit into the soft, grass-covered earth. As he raised it again he was startled by a raspy male voice coming from behind him.

"Do you know why the earth is so soft around here?"

George turned quickly, mattock raised to defend himself but lowered it to the ground as he saw Ted Sanders dressed in a well-worn, twenty-year-old, Men's Wearhouse three-piece blue pinstripe suit. George was tempted to laugh at Ted's appearance but refrained.

"Why no, Mr. Sanders. Why is the earth so soft around here?"

Ted rasped in a loud voice:

"That's because, Mr. Jackson, for near two hundred years my family plowed and cultivated this fine soil."

Ted fixed a baleful look on George as he continued.

"So your family could have work in the fields and be taken care of from birth to death. That land includes right here where we're standing."

George looked at Ted with kindness and spoke sincerely from his heart.

"Well, Mr. Sanders, way I see it, the land we're on and the bodies we're in are all just on loan from the Good Lord. But you're welcome to watch me dig for as long as you like."

That said, George turned his back to Ted and drove the mattock into the ground loosening the turf. He swung it again pulling up the earth as Ted continued to stand and watch him. George dropped the mattock and scraped earth and turf aside with his hands. He stood and looked around but Ted was gone.

CHAPTER 16

Nashville Skyline

Ted turned his old Cadillac with its two somewhat decrepit Confederate flag bumper stickers from the feeder road and onto the on-ramp for Interstate 65 north. In less than two hours he caught sight of the twin horns of the once Bell South, now the AT&T skyscraper, colloquially known as the "Batman Building," the dominant feature of the Nashville skyline. He parked in a lot near the office tower on Demonbreun Street and took the elevator to the tenth floor. Ted had shaved close, tied his conservative, striped tie in a Windsor knot, and had had his ancient suit dry-cleaned so he looked every inch a Southern aristocrat. Even his Florsheim shoes were reasonably well-polished. He thought he looked more than respectable so he was nonplussed when the receptionist, a very attractive Asian woman with immaculate, coiffed, short, gleaming black hair and costly Pierre Cardin

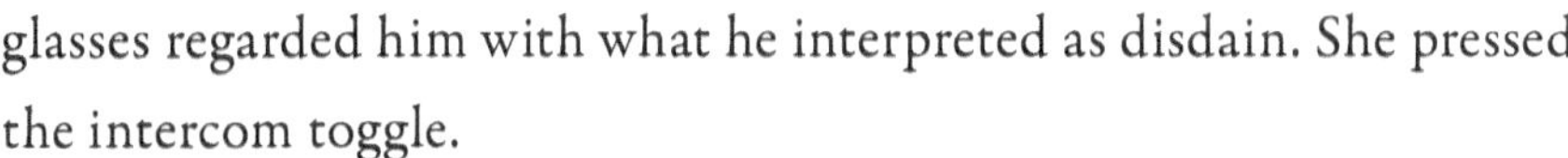

glasses regarded him with what he interpreted as disdain. She pressed the intercom toggle.

"Mr. Parks, there is a Mr. uhh . . ."

Jocelyn, for that was the name engraved on the walnut-and-brass desk wedge, looked at Ted over her glasses with an expression more appropriate for regarding a odoriferous street person than a potential client. She sensed that Ted no more belonged in the office than a skunk and for his part Ted sensed her feelings and felt such an instantaneous, intense hatred for her icy snobbishness that he controlled himself with some difficulty.

"Your name was?"

The superciliously uttered query hung in the air for a moment.

Through gritted teeth, Ted replied,

"Sanders. Ted Sanders."

"A Mr. Ted Sanders. Yes, I'll tell him."

Jocelyn opened a gilt-stamped, maroon leather day planner and made a few notes. In a slightly more polite tone and with a faint smile she said, "Mr. Parks will be with you in a few minutes. Please have a seat."

Ted heard a buzz just after he'd seated himself in the rather comfortable Chippendale-style, leather-covered, walnut armchair. Jocelyn listened to her earpiece and then looked over at Ted.

"Mr. Parks will see you now."

Ted got up and opened the heavy door with the brass knob to the left of Jocelyn's faux Louis XVI desk. He went in then immediately reemerged.

"He's in the conference room. The door to your right."

Inside the luxuriously appointed conference room with a good view of downtown Nashville and the Cumberland River, a Mozart sonata played so softly as to be almost imperceptible. Jocelyn brought in a polished silver tray complete with silver coffee pot and blue china mugs emblazoned with gold scales of justice in relief. She set it down on the massive mahogany

conference table and walked out. Ted sipped his coffee and nearly gagged for it was as strong as espresso. Immaculately urbane in his strikingly handsome, bespoke Saville Row, double-breasted, dark blue wool suit, Mason Parks, a handsome six-foot-two gentleman, in his early fifties, with an unlined face and a haircut that doubtless cost more that Ted's suit was going through the papers that Ted brought with beautifully manicured and pampered hands; his elegant, long fingers holding up each one for careful scrutiny. He finished, loosened his charcoal Sebastian Cruz necktie and fixed Ted with an appraising look. His voice was that of a federal judge pronouncing a sentence.

"Mr. Sanders, let me be frank. I only agreed to see you because my father did some work for your father. I already have far too many cases."

Ted replied sarcastically:

"I didn't drive two hours to be insulted by some snotty Oriental secretary and then be dismissed by you . . ."

With that Ted got up so abruptly and awkwardly that he knocked over a small, blue-and-white Chinese vase, which fell then shattered on the polished oak floor. Undisturbed, Mason Parks dispassionately inspected the fragments of porcelain and shrugged.

"A Chien-lung copy. It's insured. Please be seated."

Ted reseated himself but in a different chair away from the shards of the vase.

"For your information Jocelyn is Chinese."

He smiled at Ted.

"Your project will be costly."

"How costly?"

"My bank will need $57,816.47 to secure Mr. Jackson's mortgage. Then there's my fee."

"I'll have enough to cover about $70,000 total."

Mason favored Ted with a wistful smile.

"I'm sorry, Mr. Sanders. May I recommend . . ."

Ted spoke with some asperity: "If you're even half the man your father was, I want you."

Mason replied evenly: "If you were half the man your father was you could afford my fee."

"You can hold the title and I'll give you a second on my plantation."

Mason looked over a paper and shook his head somewhat sadly.

"What's left of it that is. It appears you are nearly as shaky as Mr. Jackson."

Mason picked up another document and then stared absently out the window at the Cumberland in the distance, brown with mud from a recent downpour. He continued.

"In addition to the money necessary to acquire Mr. Jackson's farm, my fee will be $25,000 with $15,000 up front as a retainer. The company will bill the rest."

Ted gasped and his face turned white as a sheet.

"I've already sent most of my family's heirlooms to auction. Some of them have been in the family passed down generation to generation for more than 200 years."

Mason Parks's face and his tone revealed a distinct lack of sympathy for Ted's family.

"Take it or leave it. Frankly, I find this type of work distasteful."

Ted sucked his gritted teeth.

"All right. Do it! Just do it! I want to see Jackson out on the street and put an end to that damned illegal animal graveyard once and for all!"

"Fine. I'll expect a cashier's check within three days."

Mason Parks stood and Ted extended his hand to seal the deal. Parks debated whether to shake Ted's hand, decided he might as well having agreed to take him on as a client and desultorily extended three very well

manicured fingers. Walking out of the conference room, Ted paused and turned to Parks.

"Young man, you may have your father's business but you don't have his values."

Parks was no more insulted than if Ted were one of the homeless people on 4th street. He stopped before a Regency mahogany mirror and admired his nearly perfect white teeth. He returned to the intercom on the conference table and flipped the toggle.

"Jocelyn. I need Aubrey at First Horizon. The old fool's going ahead with it."

"Yes, Mr. Parks."

"And you and I can discuss Mr. Sanders's suit over lunch at Jeff Ruby's."

"I'll call for a reservation."

CHAPTER 17

Brandy's Tale

S tevie set up her mobile animal healing truck on public property perilously close to Hunter's Bar thinking there was no use in "preaching
to the choir." Her signs read "CLINIC TODAY" and "HUNTING IS
MURDER" respectively. A white Ford cargo van pulled up behind the
clinic sign and a thirty-something bearded man got out wearing a sand-
colored camouflage jacket of the type issued to U.S. troops in Afghanistan
and Iraq. Stevie's heart raced expecting trouble, but the man went to the
back and opened the doors. Stevie saw an aged Golden Retriever swathed
in bloody gauze bandages. Stevie raced over and looked at the dog, ignoring
the veteran whose name was stitched in black in the jacket's breast. The man,
whose name was Sam, said in a breaking but still distinctly manly voice.

"I know she's hurt bad. Truck that hit her didn't even stop. Vet tells
me to put her down."

Stevie gazed into the retriever's limpid eyes.

"Sometimes a vet can say that a little too easily."

She proceeded to unwrap the bandages and palpate the dog's internal organs. The retriever did not object, as her touch seemed to soothe rather than causing pain. Stevie held the dog's right paw as lovingly as if the animal were her best friend suffering in agony.

"I won't lie to you, Sam is it? She's hurt real bad. Shouldn't even be riding in your van despite the pillows."

"She was my dad's dog. As long as she's here its kind of like he's still around. Can you save her, Miss Sanders?"

Stevie looked into the dog's eyes long and searchingly than sucked a breath through her teeth.

"We'll do our best to make Brandy feel better."

"How'd you know her name?"

Stevie looked at Sam and smiled.

"I read her tag."

Stevie returned to her truck and mixed a vile-looking, cloudy dark concoction and poured it into a glass jar.

As she finished pouring, Hank and Bill, both obviously under the influence, emerged from Hunter's Bar.

Unaware of the two tow truck drivers, Stevie slid some double O gelatin capsules into a paper envelope and handed it to Sam together with the dubious looking jar.

"Rub this into her joints twice a day and give her one capsule in the morning and another in the evening with food."

Sam stroked Brandy's head tenderly. Stevie looked deeply into her eyes once again as if transferring a healing energy through her stare.

"You'd better bring her back every day. No charge for life-threatening situations."

With tears in his eyes, Sam hugged Stevie hard, then pressed two twenty-dollar bills into her hand. They broke the hug and snapped their heads as the sound of Hank and Bill's wrecker approaching at speed. Bill was driving as Hank held an old Louisville Slugger baseball bat out the driver's window. He hit a home run with Stevie's "CLINIC" sign, splintering it, then swung at one of the arrow signs pointing to Stevie's tent. Hank screamed.

"Witch! You're lucky it wasn't your head! Maybe next time!"

Stevie just shook her head but Sam raced to his van and grabbed a .12 gauge riot shotgun from behind the passenger seat and racked the action. He was taking aim at the wrecker's back window when Stevie touched his shoulder as Bill gunned the engine truck tires smoking.

"What?"

"Sam, if you shot at everyone that thinks I'm a witch the county hospital would run out of beds."

"I wouldn't shoot those boys. Just scare them a little maybe."

Sam lowered the shotgun and walked to his van and put it back behind the seat. Stevie tried once more unsuccessfully to return Sam's twenties but he refused with a gesture.

"Miss Sanders, I believe in the Good Book. And I can see the Lord working through you."

Stevie smiled.

"Well, I'm not very conventional."

"Neither was Jesus."

"Bless you for saying that. Lately I've been having my doubts."

Ted had kindled a fire in the massive, nineteenth-century, five-foot wide brick fireplace. He was mumbling to himself, muttering curses about his ill treatment by Mason Parks and his uppity "zipperhead" secretary. He was stripping off his antiquated suit and referring to Parks said in a tone of such bitterness that it was strangled in acrimony.

"Got your old man's business all right."

Standing in his underwear before the blazing fire he balled up the coat, tie, vest, and trousers and fed them to the flames. Continuing to mutter he fell into a large, needlepoint-upholstered armchair and contemplated the destruction of the suit. He spoke aloud as though to the burning garments.

"A life without values ain't worth living."

George Jackson sat in a red leather-covered chair in the loan office of the Citizens Tri-County Bank holding an official threatening looking notice. The loan officer, a fifty-year-old white man, looked at him with a genuinely sympathetic expression.

"George." He began. "You've been a good customer for decades now."

George replied in a dignified tone.

"We've known each other a long time. Just give it to me straight."

"Your mortgage has been bought by a third party. You've got fifteen days to get current or they'll foreclose and take possession."

George nodded his assent and understanding and hesitatingly rose from his chair.

"Thanks. Thank you."

The loan officer's voice reflected his authentic sympathy.

"I'm sorry, George. Nothing personal. It's just the way things are these days."

He watched as George walked away with slumped shoulders and heavy almost stumbling steps. Once outside the bank George paused to catch his breath leaning against the red brick wall.

As dusk approached Ted was taking down the Confederate flag in his nightly evening ritual. He folded it as neatly and reverently as any United States marine presenting the American flag to the bereaved widow of a soldier killed in action. He kissed it with a lover's kiss and placed it in a specially constructed pine box. He turned toward the road at the sound of a truck crunching gravel. Hank and Bill's wrecker pulled up near Ted and both of them got out. Bill was smoking and chewing on one of his Swisher Sweets. He looked at Ted, and spoke respectfully with the soggy cigar still smoking.

"What can we do for you, Mr. Sanders?"

Daniel was in his Zion Sheriff's Department Dodge Ram 1500 Service Special truck cruising slowly by the white Little Souls crosses, George Jackson's house, and Stevie's trailer when the radio crackled to life as Cheryl spoke.

"Car 03. Daniel, come in please."

"03 here. Hey Cheryl. What's up?"

"What are you doing later?"

Daniel drove by Sanders Plantation and saw the H&B tow truck parked on the oval near Ted's front porch.

"Don't know. Gonna catch up with my dad, maybe at Hunter's."

"Oh. Okay. I'll be clocking out of here soon."

Daniel passed the Baptist church and as he did he sighed. Inside his church office Pastor Peter sat at his desk by candlelight with a large King James Bible open. He was writing a letter beginning in bold black capital letters, "Parishioners of Zion Baptist . . ."

CHAPTER 18

A Financial Crisis

Stevie, Gigi, and George were seated at George's yellow pine dinner table seated on pine chairs with rush seats. The repast was sparse but bountiful, consisting of a green salad with buttermilk dressing, red beans and rice, and a bowl of spaghetti. George intoned the blessing.

"Heavenly Father, bless this food to the nourishment of our bodies that we may have the strength to serve Your Will. Amen."

Stevie fervently said her Amen and they began to eat their salad when Stevie abruptly put down her fork.

"I'd like to add something. Dear God thank you for George Jackson, Amen."

George smiled and blushed. Stevie resumed enjoying her salad but George bowed his head and sat silently. Stevie became concerned and set down her fork once more.

"George, are you all right?"

George walked to a kitchen drawer and pulled out an official looking envelope and handed it to Stevie without a word. Stevie took it, opened it and was shocked by its import.

"This is terrible."

George sounded uncharacteristically glum.

"The worst part is I have nobody to blame but myself. Feel like I've let you down. I'm sorry, I really am."

Stevie replied with a degree of heat.

"You've never given up on anything in your life. Don't start now."

George gave her a wistful, slightly sad smile.

"Do you know where I can lay my hands on $60,000 because I don't."

George paused.

"Otherwise I have less than fifteen days to find a buyer. At least that way we can find some cheap land and start over."

Stevie bridled.

"But this land has been in your family for generations. Your folks are buried here. Your family."

She looked at George and said with sincerity:

"I'll find the money somehow."

George rose from his chair and put his arms around her from behind and hugged her long and hard.

"You just remember that you and Gigi mean a whole lot more to me than this land. You hear me, girl?"

"I hear you."

Stevie had heard him, believed him, but felt something different. An upwelling of the love a loving daughter feels for her father. She rose and the two of them hugged once more. A gust of wind rattled one of the windowpanes. Gigi got up to look.

Ted was closing the door after Hank and Bill left and he watched as the wrecker drove away from the house. He walked to the kitchen table where a bottle of Jack Daniel's stood by three empty glasses. Choosing one he remembered was his he filled the tumbler nearly to the rim and slugged it down then poured another brimmer as a sudden gust of wind came through an open window.

CHAPTER 19

A Night at the Frist

The Frist Museum was hosting an exhibition celebrating young Tennessee artists and Mason Parks was in attendance on opening night accompanied by Jocelyn. Both were dressed in fine quality evening clothes. Jocelyn was wearing a blue Givenchy dress and a string of matching, eight-millimeter natural pearls adorned her neck. She sniggered.

"Mr. Sanders called twice this morning. I put him on permanent hold."

She handed Mason a pink memo with Ted's number. He took an iPhone from a pocket inside his Saville Row suit jacket and dialed.

"Jocelyn, you're cruel. I enjoy that in a woman."

Ted answered.

"Mr. Sanders, this is Mason Parks. Now calm down. You want what? Yes, yes we can certainly get you a fair hearing. But it's a risk. All right then."

He pressed the phone then looked at Jocelyn with an expression more amused than bemused.

"Call Steven Hill. It seems we have a custody case. Now he wants his granddaughter."

Jocelyn was startled and offended.

"You'd allow a child to live with that old redneck?"

"Now, Jocelyn, Ted Sanders is a ruined, aristocratic redneck. There is a difference."

Jocelyn remained unconvinced.

"If you say so."

"Besides, as long as he has any assets worth pursuing, he's a client."

Jocelyn arched her full black eyebrows.

"If you say so."

Then both simultaneously burst out laughing to the discomfiture of several shocked, effete art aficionados nearby.

That same evening, Stevie was driving along the main highway near Zion, assuming one could call the two-lane road a highway, carefully searching the shoulder. She spotted a dark mass a hundred yards ahead and pulled over. She pressed the button on the steering column to turn on the emergency flashers and got out. Using a rubber dustpan Stevie scooped up the road-killed barn owl and deftly flipped it into a plastic Piggly Wiggly bag.

Pastor Peter was putting the finishing touches on his Sunday sermon. When he finished he left his computer, stood and faced his office mirror and began to practice his delivery.

"Parishioners of Zion Baptist. This Sunday's sermon is on a subject of special meaning in these challenging times. The true meaning and true value of spirituality."

Stevie returned to her trailer in George's yard and entered with the plastic bag now heavy with owl. She unfolded a red leatherette metal card table, sheeted it with a plastic garbage bag and opened the Piggly Wiggly bag. The aroma of several days dead owl made her wrinkle her nose. She opened a jar of Vicks® VapoRub™ and delicately applied some next to each nostril. She struck a kitchen match and lit two fragrant wax candles, then lit two joss sticks of sandalwood incense. The red LED letters on the radio alarm clock read 9:30 pm. Stevie donned a pair of rubber surgical gloves and removed a huge dead raven along with the owl. She sprayed both birds with a plastic spray bottle marked 'disinfectant'. She reverently smoothed the owl's blood-matted feathers and murmured a prayer.

"Dear God, bless this creature, bless his soul. I thank you for all the beauty he gave to the world and I ask you to forgive me for what I'm about to do."

Stevie looked into the dulled, almost opaque, once golden eyes of the owl and continued.

"I'm so sorry. We really do need the money."

She pulled the largest feathers from the wings and carefully laid them out according to length; then taking a garden shear, skillfully amputated each dangerously taloned foot. She wrapped the remains in cheesecloth, went to the sink and washed her ungloved hands over and over. Gigi slept through the dismemberment of both creatures. Stevie took her cell phone and pressed keys. Pastor Peter answered.

"Peter, sorry it's late. I have a strange request. I need to be baptized again."

Duncan Hunter arrived in the parking lot of his eponymous bar early in the morning, sipping coffee, chewing on a donut and listening to FOX talk radio. He emerged from the driver's seat only to find "HUNTING IS MURDER" flyers tacked with a staple gun to the pine four-by-fours and all over the west side of the building. Furious, he dropped both coffee and donut and began to tear them down, crumpling them.

Stevie was carefully and meticulously wrapping owl and crow talons for shipping. She slid them gently into a USPS Priority box and affixed a label reading "Sorcerers Supply: 11289 Highway 1: Miami, Florida."

That evening Ted sat in his darkened den at a old walnut partner's desk piled high with various papers, bills, and manila envelopes. The bald eagle mount up atop the bookcase was now missing all of its tail feathers and its left talon; the absence of the latter made the eagle stand at an odd precarious angle. The feathers and talon were encased in a large Ziplock bag. He put his fountain pen to a long letter and signed it. He filled out a Federal Express slip with his information and then the recipient which read: U.S. Fish and Wildlife Service: Office of Law Enforcement: 5275 Leesburg Pike, Falls Church, Virginia. He placed the letter and the plastic bag in a FedEx box then sealed it.

The morning after the opening at the Frist, Mason Parks was speaking to a young man dressed in expensive black jeans.

"Steven, we need evidence on our client's daughter, Stephanie Sanders. For starters we need to establish that her residence is unfit for human habitation. Particularly for a child."

Steven Hill was taking notes as Mason described Stevie's trailer and her menagerie.

"Relax, Mr. Parks. This is too easy."

Steven picked up his worn leather briefcase and excused himself as Jocelyn exchanged a look with Mason Parks.

At the Zion Baptist Church Pastor Peter was readying Stevie for the second baptism she had asked him for. She was wearing a white robe over her habitual torn worn jeans and flannel shirt. Pastor Peter looked deeply into her eyes.

"Are you ready for this?"

"I need this. I feel tainted deep in my soul."

The pastor led her outside and they walked together to the stream behind the church. The stream was swollen from a recent rain and the water was cold as Stevie stepped in. She shuddered involuntarily. Further downstream was a depression in which the water was four feet deep. The two made their way stepping carefully to avoid slipping on the numerous flat rocks. They stopped at the edge of the deeper water and both were cold and wet. He placed his right hand in the small of her back and bent her over immersing her backward in the water.

"I baptize thee in the name of the Father, and of the Son, and of the Holy Ghost, amen."

He then raised her as she shook her head and spluttered. He kissed her lips and embraced her passionately.

Sheriff Olsen was at the Sanders Plantation aiming Ted's vintage Winchester Model 94 30–30 rifle at a water-filled, plastic gallon jug set on a rise about a hundred yards off. He aimed carefully, squeezed the trigger, fired, and missed as Ted observed him.

"Something needs adjusting. Maybe it's me."

"Weapon's in perfect condition."

Sheriff Olsen handed the rifle to Ted who put it to his shoulder, aimed carefully, fired and was shocked to see the jug intact.

"Maybe it's both of us."

Ted reddened. He worked the lever quickly and fired again and again until on the fifth round the jug exploded.

Steve Hill's light gray BMW X3 sped away from Stevie's trailer after smearing dog shit and other animal feces on the seat of Gigi's swing. The colorful plastic sandbox was dotted with piles of feces and one sneaker Gigi had left out was mashed into a runny brown deposit. He had thoroughly documented the unsanitary condition of the yard and Gigi's play areas. His Canon digital camera lay on the passenger seat of the BMW.

Cheryl was on her computer in the Zion Sheriff's office when she heard the printer and walked over to it. The tray had a fax incoming. The cover sheet had an official logo of a duck flying from a mountain lake with the sun over a mountain in the distance. Printed near the logo was "U.S. Fish & Wildlife Service. Office of Law Enforcement" the text read.

"Please apprehend one Stephanie Sanders suspected of illegal trafficking of eagle feathers and raptor components."

Stevie's details followed. Cheryl snatched up the fax and after returning to her computer to research the relevant federal laws, ran out the station door to the parking lot in the rear where Daniel was about to get into his patrol car. Cheryl's tone was flat and devoid of any familiarity.

"It looks like your high school sweetheart is in big trouble."

She handed him the papers and he glanced at the cover sheet and whistled.

"Damn, this is serious."

He added,

"And she's not my old sweetheart."

Cheryl's voice softened.

"Sorry. Would you care to buy a lonely girl a drink at Hunter's?"

"Come on now, Cheryl, at Hunter's bar? I . . ."

"Never mind. Here I've been online all day in case you wanted to rescue one of your old girlfriends."

Daniel smiled.

"All day?"

Without a reply she handed him a folder.

"I'll see you later."

She flashed him a warm smile.

"Maybe we should show these to my dad . . . together."

She headed back to the front door followed by Daniel.

"Just be ready for trouble though. The boys at Hunter's may not take kindly."

Cheryl decided to leave and walked to her red Chevy Spark.

"Well, you'll be there to protect me now won't you?"

Daniel opened the driver's door with a grin. Cheryl got in and he closed it.

CHAPTER 20

An Afternoon at Hunter's Bar

Sheriff Olsen sat at the epoxy-resin-coated bar halfway through a cheeseburger and a side of wedge cut French fries. Bill and Hank were at the end throwing down a couple of thick glass mugs of Budweiser as Duncan wiped down the counter with a rag. Hank addressed Duncan who continued polishing the bar.

"You see that Sanders girl just up the road?"

Duncan nodded noncommittally. He looked over at the sheriff who was washing down the last of the burger with black coffee.

Duncan spoke without enthusiasm.

"Uh-huh."

Hank said in an aggrieved, complaining tone:

"She's plastering antihunting signs all over the county. Worse than ever." Bill added forcefully.

"We got our eye on her."

Hank shot a warning look to Bill as Daniel entered the bar accompanied by Cheryl. Duncan left off his wiping as the bar chatter ceased abruptly. Bill and Hank simply stared at Cheryl who favored them with a big smile. She and Daniel walked over to the sheriff who slid off his barstool and stood with a surprised look at the two.

"Daniel. Miss Cheryl. What a surprise."

"Dad, we have a problem. It's Stevie Sanders. She may have broken a federal law by selling eagle feathers and parts."

Sheriff Olsen and Duncan made knowing eye contact as Duncan nodded.

"I can't say I'm surprised. Unlike my youngest son here and his brother too I suppose, I never liked her."

Daniel looked first at his father then at Cheryl and said in a pain-filled voice as he remembered several unpleasant, awkward instances.

"Dad. We were fifteen."

Duncan watched the sheriff and his son then looked at Daniel.

"Daniel, what will you have?"

Daniel looked from Duncan to Cheryl.

"Way I was brought up, Duncan, it was always ladies first."

Hank and Bill eyed Cheryl with an odd mixture of lust and hate.

Duncan realized his error.

"Excuse me . . . ma'am."

"A Black Jack straight up, please."

Duncan nodded his approval of the request. Hank and Bill shot a nasty look at the bar owner. The ugly look was not lost on Daniel. He eyed Hank who looked away though Bill did not drop his gaze but continued

to stare fixedly while alternating between smoking and chewing his soggy, Swisher Sweet cigar.

"Make that two," said Daniel.

Sheriff Olsen looked at his son with a dubious and critical expression. The sheriff eyed the two tumblers of Jack Daniel's that Duncan set down on the table in front of his son and his secretary.

"Is that so," said the sheriff in a bemused tone.

"She's become an expert on eagles."

Daniel handed his father the folder with Fish & Wildlife Department regulations. The sheriff read them and said,

"Five thousand dollars per feather plus six months in prison. This is insane. Eagles are nothing but better-dressed vultures."

Cheryl said to Daniel:

"Ten eagle feathers could cost your ex five years in Federal prison plus a $50,000 fine."

Daniel glared at her. Cheryl tossed down the drink in one go.

The sheriff, impressed by Cheryl's drinking ability, said sarcastically:

"Another brilliant law from the Feds in D.C."

He looked at Daniel.

"So exactly what do you propose to do about Ms. Sanders?"

"I can arrest her or talk with her, but at this point I'd say we give her the benefit of the doubt."

The sheriff looked at his son.

"You would. I say you investigate the hell out of her. Otherwise we may have the Federal boys visiting Zion."

"That's ridiculous."

"Find the time to deal with it or I'll do it myself."

Daniel nodded his affirmation. The sheriff looked at Cheryl.

"Hope you didn't start my son drinking again."

Cheryl looked at the sheriff, then at Daniel and finally at Hank and Bill.

"Think I've had enough of the local color. You . . . ?"

"I think I'm gonna hang out for a while."

Cheryl got the message.

"Okay. You have a good night Daniel. Sheriff."

"You too," said Daniel in a pleasant tone.

Daniel watched her shapely form the entire way out of Duncan's then he left the table for the bar and asked for another Jack.

CHAPTER 21

Investigating an Eagle

Daniel parked his patrol truck in the oval drive in front of the Sanders house. It was dusk and the tattered Confederate flag still drooped from its pole in the still humid air. He looked at the flag with a degree of disgust that was visible on his face. He walked to the old wooden door with the paint cracked and peeling. He pushed the doorbell and when that was not answered, lifted the heavy horseshoe brass knocker and let it fall three times. There was still no response so he removed his black leather, lead-filled sap and struck the door three times releasing a miniature shower of paint chips. The door opened a crack and Ted Sanders wearing an old, stained, white embroidered dressing gown peered out.

"What is it?" he snarled.

"I'm looking for Stevie."

"Stevie who?"

"Stephanie Sanders. Your daughter."

Ted looked hard at Daniel.

"Do I know you? Now I remember. You're Sheriff Olsen's boy, the one who ran off with his brother's wife."

Daniel was momentarily taken aback and said in a less than authoritative voice:

"Do you know where I might find her? It's important."

Ted continued to stare hard into Daniel's eyes, recollection and recognition dawning in his own bleary bloodshot eyes.

"Now I remember. I caught you two in the barn. Already had your shirts off and your hands were all over her little titties. Good thing I showed up when I did. Lord only knows what would have happened. I whaled the living tar out of her for that. I recollect the sheriff whipped your skinny butt so hard you didn't sit down for a week."

Daniel's voice indicated that he remembered the incident only too well and when he spoke it was as if he were fourteen again.

"I don't see how that's relevant, I ah . . ."

Ted was triumphant and he knew it.

"You've spent your life messing girls up, boy. And right now you're cheapening that gold badge. Now get off my property. And if you want to find Stephanie try her down at Jackson's nigger digs at the other end of the world."

Daniel sighed, thoroughly nonplussed by Ted's tirade and his own boyhood memories. He turned away without a word and walked to his patrol vehicle.

Stevie was in her trailer taking a large, road-killed raven out of a Piggly Wiggly bag when George knocked on her door, startling her so much so that she dropped the bird. George opened the unlocked door and entered as a sheepish and embarrassed Stevie picked up the raven by its feet.

"Got any coffee on?" he asked.

"In the kitchen. Help yourself."

George walked to the coffeemaker and poured a cup from the glass carafe as Stevie slid the bird back in the bag.

"Called all my close and distant relatives today. Won't be able to raise enough money to save the farm that way. Felt bad just asking."

"I'm working on some ways too."

"We're running out of time, Stevie. Might have to start thinking about other places to go. Don't know what will happen to Little Souls."

"We might be able to stay at the church for a while if it came to that."

"Pastor Peter got an extra room or two?"

Stevie nodded,

"Yeah. But things could get a little complicated with Peter and all."

George hesitated for a long moment then took a deep breath.

"Stevie. This has never been any of my business but you're family and living here with me now. Why'd you ever get mixed up with a minister in the first place if he reminds you of everything you don't like about your father?"

CHAPTER 22

Broken Glass at Duncan's

As the sun began to rise in Zion, a shadowy figure raised its right arm and threw a heavy rock at Duncan's front window. It sailed right through the gold lettering reading "Hunter's Bar" shattering the entire pane. This first rock was quickly followed by another equally large stone, which bounced off the rough pine siding and fell on the porch. The second one had a paper wrapped around it secured with a green rubber band.

Red lights flashed in the dawn from Daniel's patrol vehicle in front of Hunter's. Daniel was examining shards of glass and took a snapshot of the window and damage with his iPhone. Duncan Hunter was sweeping up glass with a corn broom into a rubber dustpan. Duncan left

off sweeping and picked up the rock with the paper and freed it from the rubber band. He read it red faced. The note read in capital letters, "HUNTING KILLS!"

"That crazy witch. Now she's trying to kill me."

Daniel pointed out the obvious.

"You weren't even here."

Duncan put down the rock and walked inside to the bar. He pulled a civilian version of the Russian AK47 rifle with a thirty-round magazine. Daniel saw him and spoke in a commanding tone, which stopped him before he had taken three steps.

"Put that away! Don't even think about it or I swear I'll place you under arrest!"

Duncan replaced the rifle rather sheepishly.

"I demand police protection!"

"Fine. I'll ask the sheriff. Now sweep up all this glass before someone steps on it and gets hurt." Daniel's patrol was about to pull away when Sheriff Olsen arrived braking hard and releasing a shower of gravel, blue lights flashing. The sheriff got out and heaved a sigh. He looked at Daniel.

"Your animal loving friend Stevie is becoming a real menace."

"I'm not convinced she had anything to do with it. Duncan here's requesting police protection."

"He's a silly old woman."

Daniel handed his father the paper. The sheriff read it.

"I've seen her antihunting signs. They're all over Zion. Looks like your old girlfriend Sanders has struck again."

"It wasn't exactly a pipe bomb."

The sheriff nodded, folded the note, which he placed in his breast pocket. He walked to his patrol car, turned, and said in a conversational voice:

"And Daniel, tell her to stop with the no hunting crusade. Hunters have guns and like to kill things. I do too. There hasn't been a homicide around here for quite awhile and I aim to keep it that way."

"That's right. Hunters have feelings too . . ."

CHAPTER 23

Ted and Peter

That afternoon, Pastor Peter was delighted with his horse. The beautiful animal was gaiting perfectly as only a pure-bred and well-trained Tennessee walking horse can. Ted approached the outdoor arena without a word and stood quietly for some time as Peter came around the bend and noticed him.

"Now that's what I call one fine Tennessee walker."

Peter dismounted.

"Ted. How have you been? I'm surprised to see you out and about."

"Reverend, I need your guidance."

He locked his eyes on the man of God's.

"You're the only person in Zion I can trust."

At this statement, Peter paled.

"The only man that speaks the same language I do."

"I assume you're referring to the language of faith."

"In thee O' Lord, do I put my trust. Let me never be ashamed; deliver me in Thy righteousness."

"Psalm 31," said Peter

"I've been troubled, Reverend."

"What's been bothering you?"

"I've been thinking long and hard about what it means to take an eye for an eye."

"I see. The best thing we can do is to bow our heads together, and pray."

Pastor Peter began the prayer.

"Dear Father, blessed be us sinners through Your forgiveness."

Ted raised his head and said tersely:

"I can't . . . I just can't continue."

Without another word Ted walked away quickly leaving Pastor Peter genuinely nonplussed.

Stevie used a staple gun to tack her signs onto telephone poles on the roadside perilously close to Hunter's Bar. She returned to her truck and opened her green medical supplies plastic box. It was empty.

"Shoot!"

She got in the truck and quickly drove off.

Angel Wells, an attractive, bespectacled, forty-year-old woman with a severe bun temporarily imprisoning her long auburn hair was sitting at her desk in the county children's services office looking horror struck at the color glossy images of the yard near Stevie's trailer. An opened manila envelope addressed to "Children's Services" marked in bold red Sharpie "Open Immediately," lay on the metal frame office desk. She carefully put the images back in the envelope and placed it in a file headed "Gabriella Sanders." She picked up an ink stamp with a shaking, well-manicured hand, and stamped "Urgent" in big, block, red letters several times on the file.

A man dressed in denim jeans and a flannel hunter's shirt shook a red plastic gasoline jug against Stevie's sign, stepped away and threw a lit kitchen match at it. The sign burst into flames. He doused each corner of Stevie's tent then threw another match leaving the tent burning fiercely.

Stevie hopped from her truck and checked her mailbox and saw an envelope from Sorcerer's Supply. She ripped it open and grabbed a check for $500, which she folded and put into her jeans pocket. Inside her trailer she took medical instruments, medications, lotions, and gauze and hurriedly put then in her box.

Daniel's patrol truck with red lights flashing was parked behind what little remained of Stevie's tent. Daniel was sifting through the ashes as Stevie pulled up.

"Station got a call five minutes ago about a fire alongside of the road."

Stevie was in shock.

"Why would anyone want to burn down my tent?"

Daniel asked,

"So you have no idea who would do this?"

Stevie quickly recovered from her initial shock and dissolved into anger. She said acidly.

"Like maybe every customer of Hunter's Bar."

"Well, excuse me for saying it but what did you expect? And by the way someone threw rocks through Duncan's windows."

She replied in a combative and belligerent tone:

"Yeah. So what?"

"One of them had a note wrapped around it that said "Hunting Is Murder." Where were you early this morning?"

Stevie smiled, tight-lipped and shook her head.

"I have a great little alibi."

Daniel flipped open a notepad.

"And what might that be?"

"Gigi, my five-year-old daughter."

"I'll take her word for it but I seriously doubt Duncan Hunter will."

"There were those two good old boys from H&B wrecking driving a pickup that threatened me the other day after they whacked my signs with a baseball bat."

"This situation is getting a bit more serious."

"It didn't seem all that serious at the time."

Daniel made notes.

"Why did you have to pitch your tent so close to obvious trouble?"

"I keep hoping I might win a convert. No sense preaching to the choir."

Daniel said blandly:

"And what do you know about any eagle parts being sold through the mail?"

Stevie was taken aback. Her voice reflected surprise and consternation.

"What are you talking about?"

Daniel shrugged his shoulders and said diffidently.

"I'll need to come over to your trailer and clinic and check some things out. Am I going to need a warrant?"

Stevie hesitated a moment.

"Well, well no."

"Meanwhile the sheriff asked me to ask you politely if you could cool it with the antihunting crusade until we determine exactly what is going on."

Daniel leaned down and picked up the still moist end of a well-chewed little cigar. He regarded it with disgust.

"I think I know the two idiots you were talking about. I'll look them up."

Stevie brightened.

"Swell."

Daniel was headed back to his patrol vehicle when he turned.

"Stevie, word's around town that you and George Jackson may be looking for a new home."

"Not if I can help it."

Daniel spoke with genuine feeling in his voice.

"If you need anything, anything at all let me know."

Stevie did not reply but stood silently and ruefully, contemplating the charred remains of her healing tent.

Daniel was in Hunter's Bar questioning Duncan about Hank and Bill.

"No, I haven't seen those boys yet. They usually start drinking around three, that is if they're not working, which is usually most of the time."

"Well if you do, tell them to call the station."

"What's this about anyway?"

"Somebody torched Stevie Sanders's signs and tent."

"You mean the animal rights slut? The minister's mistress?"

Daniel was totally taken aback. Duncan noticed his consternation and continued.

"Hey! It's no secret. The whole county knows. Everyone except her father, and that's because he don't talk to no one."

"More likely he don't listen to anyone."

"Well I'm sure she threw those rocks through my windows."

Daniel shook his head vigorously.

"I know her and I can almost guarantee you she didn't do it."

Duncan looked skeptical but decided to say nothing. Daniel was the sheriff's son, no Luke to be sure but an Olsen notwithstanding, and so worthy of Duncan's respect, even if he had come to his bar with a nigger girl.

CHAPTER 24

Muffy's Revenge

Stevie spent a good thirty minutes carefully applying makeup and lipstick. She combed her rebellious blond hair into a semblance of order then contemplated her one gray cotton blouse and the gray, long cotton skirt, both of which had been on a super sale at Walmart. She reappraised her look in the mirror and smiled with satisfaction. She hadn't dressed so conservatively since Luke's funeral. In less than twenty minutes she parked next to Lucille Abbott's gleaming black Lincoln. As she exited her mud-spattered truck she was surprised to see the American flag flying at half-staff and wondered who had died. She rang the doorbell and Ezekiel answered.

"Good morning. Is Mrs. Abbott in?"

Ezekiel smiled.

"And a good morning to you, Ms. Sanders."

At the end of the formal hall, Stevie could see a large and very well executed painting of a porcine tabby cat, the late lamented Muffy. Unseen, Lucille Abbott called from another room in an irritable, confrontational tone as if anyone would dare to darken her door.

"Who's there?"

Stevie answered in a smaller than usual voice.

"It's Stevie Sanders, ma'am."

Lucille walked over to the door dressed in mourning clothes with black lace gloves. She eyed Stevie suspiciously and her disdain was written all over her unlined but aged face as she saw Stevie's worn cowboy boots whose pointed toes peered out from her long dress. Stevie coughed gently, then began.

"I'm sorry to disturb you but it's about Little Souls."

Lucille looked confused.

"Whatever are you talking about?"

Stevie said hurriedly.

"The bank is foreclosing on George's land. The cemetery, Muffy's eternal resting place."

Her voice rose almost breaking.

"It's all in danger."

As Stevie spoke a beautiful, light gray Persian kitten pushed against Lucille's right leg purring loudly.

"Why are you telling me this?"

Now it was Stevie's turn to be confused.

"May I come in?"

Lucille said imperiously:

"Why no you can't. I don't invite my servants to dinner and I don't invite strangers into my home."

Stevie was shocked at this antebellum behavior in such a polished, educated, and sophisticated woman.

"You don't ever eat with Ezekiel?"

Lucille's forehead previously unlined, wrinkled and her luxurious brown eyebrows arched.

"Good heavens no, child. Proper boundaries are the very foundation of a civil society."

Though astonished by such an aristocratic and distinctly undemocratic attitude, Stevie was determined to do her best to save George's property and so she pressed on doggedly.

"I see. All right, let me come to the point. George needs $60,000 to save Little Souls."

Lucille raised her eyebrows even higher.

"You're asking me for $60,000?"

"It's not charity. He'll pay you interest on the money. You'd be just like a bank."

This was an unfortunate comparison and Lucille became not just annoyed but angry. She said in a stentorian tone, gesturing with a well-manicured right hand beringed with costly jewels indicating the Abbott mansion.

"Young lady, does this, do I look like a bank?"

She picked up the beautiful kitten and continued.

"You see before you a house in mourning. You see our flag at half-staff then you ask me for money? And at such a time this seems like a reasonable and proper request to you?"

Chastened, Stevie spoke in an uncharacteristically meek voice.

"I'm sorry. I just thought Muffy would . . ."

Lucille seized on Stevie's former words, remembering how Stevie had had the audacity, the unmitigated gall to school her at Muffy's funeral. The payback was ever so sweet to her mind. She said in a pseudo sweet voice:

"Roast in the fiery furnace?"

Stevie knew there was absolutely no use in continuing trying to make Lucille understand that at the time she spoke those fateful words she was only trying to help the distraught older woman. Summoning up a hitherto deliberately suppressed reserve of self-respect, she said with quiet dignity:

"I'm very sorry to have disturbed you, Mrs. Abbott. I'll not trouble you further."

She turned to go. Not content with making Stevie eat her funerary words, Lucille could not resist taking down someone she saw as an arrogant, liberated, young woman even further.

"How you Sanders have managed to go from patricians to paupers in less than three generations is beyond me. I actually feel sorry for you."

She added wickedly.

"That is almost."

The door closed after Stevie with a distinct click. On her way out she resisted the strong temptation to spit on the Lincoln's gleaming hood not to spare the finish on the car but only because it would only make extra work for Ezekiel.

CHAPTER 25

More Trouble

A Zion County official Ford Taurus in regulation white was parked directly in front of Stevie's trailer. Angel Wells was in the middle of being besieged by Stevie's menagerie and was trying unsuccessfully to scrape dog shit from her new black leather right shoe with a matchbook. She shook off a shaggy, rather large sheepdog mix and made it to the trailer's door followed by the dog. She knocked sharply and as there was no answer she pounded on it more out of frustration at her shoe being defiled than in accordance with the performance of her official duties. Nearly in tears, she punched a text on her iPhone, then hurried to her car followed by the dog and drove off trying to avoid running over the dog, which had taken such a liking to her that it continued to run alongside the Taurus.

Daniel had located a local taxidermist who had a reputation as someone knowledgeable concerning both raptors and federal laws regarding

possession and sale of eagle feathers and parts, through John Shaw, the Zion county wildlife officer. He was standing on the porch of the man's home. They had finished speaking and after shaking hands, the taxidermist handed Daniel several small manila envelopes.

Stevie left George's house with Gigi in her arms and to her surprise, Sheriff Olsen's patrol vehicle was parked behind her trailer with the sheriff inside. Seeing her, the sheriff opened the door and donned his hat then waited next to the car.

"Gigi, honey, can you play on Grandpa George's porch for a little while?"

"Okay, Mommy."

"I'll be right back."

Stevie walked back to the sheriff. Fortunately, Gigi had not spotted him.

"Why Sheriff Olsen, what brings you out here?"

"Stephanie Sanders. You have been served."

With that the sheriff handed her a legal document. Stevie read it. The sheriff touched his right hand to his hat in the courtly Southern manner. He said somewhat regretfully:

"I told my son all this animal rights stuff would backfire on you somehow."

He nodded his head to Stevie, who stood still in a mild state of shock. As the sheriff drove off she reread the paper with the large, black block capital lettering: "NOTICE TO APPEAR."

Later that day Pastor Peter was lighting candles in the church when he heard loud knocking on the west side door. He opened it to find a flustered Stevie and knew immediately that something was seriously amiss.

"What is it? Is there something wrong?"

Without a word she handed him the Notice to Appear. Then on the verge of tears she spoke breathlessly.

"Now they're trying to take Gigi away from me."

The pastor was incredulous.

"This is utterly absurd. I'll just appear with you and it will be over before it begins."

"And just how do you figure that?"

"I can personally attest to the fact that you are a great mother."

"And how exactly are you supposed to know that?"

"I'm the minister of the Zion Baptist Church. They'll believe me."

Stevie almost shrieked in frustration.

"Peter, you're delusional. The whole town knows I don't even attend your church!"

Peter thought for a moment than made a decision. He spoke decisively.

"Then I'll just have to tell them the truth about us."

"How is that going to prove I'm a good parent for God's sake? Or even a good person for that matter? Think about it."

Stevie took Peter's face in her rather cold and sweaty hands.

"I came to you because I love you and because you're her father. But you can't really be there. It's dangerous. For all of us."

"I'll hire the best lawyer in the county."

"I don't want a lawyer. I don't know anything about them other than they are trouble no matter what and damned expensive. Bringing a lawyer will just make me look guilty, like I've got something to hide."

"They won't take Gigi away. She doesn't have anyone but you."

"When I got back to my trailer the other day someone had spread animal filth all over the yard."

"What's this all about? Tell me what's going on."

"Somebody is going through a whole lot of trouble to make me look like an unfit mother."

Peter smiled knowingly.

"Of course there's one easy way to solve this entire problem."

He added confidently:

"And it's legal."

Stevie looked at him with hope in her eyes.

"Stevie, all that's happening is a sign that it's time we became a true family in the eyes of both God and man."

Stevie shook her head wistfully and spoke into his ear in a whisper.

"Peter, to me, our relationship exists in its own beautiful world, its own beautiful private world. It doesn't need to be put on public display."

"Stevie, being my wife in the eyes of the Lord and the community isn't necessarily such a bad thing."

Stevie was now both frustrated, anxious, and irritated. She spoke somewhat stridently.

"When will you ever understand that I could never marry a man who uses his religion to rule over somebody else's life? I grew up watching my father slowly make my mother disappear, then she died."

Peter replied with more heat than was wise given Stevie's position. He had overplayed his hand and rather than recognizing that he was on the verge of delivering an irrecoverable and fatal blow to their relationship. He was so desperate to legalize his marital status with Stevie and Gigi that he invoked her tortured relationship with Ted.

"Stevie, your whole life has been one big reaction against everything you hate about your father, You think that you're better than all that but the very things you despise about him control everything you do, everything you believe in, and all the people around you are suffering because if it."

Stevie turned away in a rage, ran to the door without a word, and slammed it so hard on the way out that the rafters rattled.

CHAPTER 26

Birds of a Feather

D aniel was communicating with Cheryl over the police radio, as cell service in Zion was less than full coverage, especially in the more isolated areas.

"So what'd you find out about the wrecker boys?"

He was pulling into George Jackson's driveway, passing the miniature Flanders Fields cemetery of Little Souls when Cheryl responded.

"H&B Wrecker Service. Owned by Hank Block and Bill Spicer. That cigar you found . . ."

"Yeah?"

"Well it wasn't a Swisher Sweet but a Davidoff Nicaraguan robusto. Can't get one in too many places but I found a store over in Pulaski that sells them. That's Spicer's hometown."

"10–4 on that. Good work. Hey I'm pulling into Stevie Sanders now, Call you later."

"10–4 over and out. You'd better."

Gigi was tugging at her pant leg as Stevie fed a kitten with one of Gigi's old baby bottles. Daniel knocked politely on the screen door of the trailer. Stevie was glad to see him.

"Hey you," she said.

Daniel opened the door holding a cardboard box. He looked at Stevie who smiled than down at Gigi who hid behind her mother and peeked out to stare at his uniform and pistol.

"Hey, Stevie, what's your little one's name again?"

"Gigi."

Daniel saw a large feather standing vertically, caught between stoppered glass bottles containing colored powders and clear liquids and an old marble mortar and pestle. He put the box down on a nearly shelf and picked up the feather looking it over closely. Stevie watched him.

"This looks like a . . ."

"Wing feather from a barn owl. The poor thing got hit by a car about a week ago on route 11."

"I guess he wasn't so wise after all."

Daniel replaced the feather, opened the cardboard box, and removed a talon. He handed it to Stevie without saying a word.

"That's the right talon from a large raven."

He took back the raven's foot and handed her a feather. She examined it for less than five seconds.

"Tail feather from a Great Horned owl."

Daniel handed her a much larger talon and Stevie gasped.

"Oh my God. That's a golden eagle's claw. They're completely illegal unless you're a Native American or it's been in your family for a long while and it's a federal felony to sell one. My father has a stuffed one in his study. Where'd you get this anyway?"

Daniel took it from her and rolled it in his hand over and over.

"You know there's a big underground business in animal parts, especially endangered species. Sick people with a lot of money who use elixirs, stuff from witch doctors, and participate in dark magic rituals."

Daniel looked around the room and at Stevie's worktable seeing the medical instruments including clippers and shears.

"Tell me. Do you have any real enemies?"

Stevie shrugged her shoulders, as if to say: "Who doesn't"?

"Can you think of anyone who might turn you into the Department of Fish and Wildlife for selling eagle parts?"

Stevie was genuinely shocked and her face and body reflected the impact of Daniel's question. She stuttered.

"I, . . . No. No."

She looked down at Gigi who was still fascinated by Daniel, his sinister black automatic pistol, and shiny gold star.

"Honey, could you go play in the bedroom for awhile?"

Gigi stopped staring and tore off toward the bedroom.

"Daniel. You know George is about to lose the farm. Ever since we found that out, well, I've been clipping the talons from some birds for money."

Daniel gave her a hard stare.

"But I swear to God no eagles. I swear it."

Daniel's gaze softened and he nodded.

"I think maybe someone's trying to frame you."

Stevie opened a drawer and handed Daniel the Notice to Appear. He read it.

"This could be just a coincidence."

Stevie said, the incredulity manifesting in her tone:

"And all of a sudden the bank's foreclosing on George's property?"

"So you're thinking something's up all the way around?"

"Seems like the more I've been trying to pull all the pieces of my life together, the more they've been flying apart."

"I believe you about the feathers and claws. But that's about all I can offer you."

Daniel hesitated then continued.

"For now."

He put the bird parts back in the cardboard box and made ready to leave. Stevie stopped him and put her hand on his arm.

"You could come to the custody hearing."

"Might be possible."

"It never hurts to have a cop on your side."

Daniel smiled at her and there was warmth in it as he remembered her at fourteen.

"No I suppose it doesn't. But I've already been standing up for you with the sheriff so don't let me down. I got my own problems."

She let go of his arm and he turned away to leave.

"Daniel. I have a question."

He turned back.

"You've known me longer than almost anybody."

Daniel nodded affirmatively. She continued.

"Do you think my whole life I've just been trying not to be like my dad?"

Daniel spoke noncommittally.

"I don't know. I really don't."

He looked her in the eye for a long moment and in his eyes she could see pain, confusion, and inconsolable loss. He left and she sagged into the lone cushioned chair in the trailer.

CHAPTER 27

The Best Laid Plans

Stevie and Gigi walked into George's house that evening to find George slumped in his ancient, wrinkled, brown Naugahyde easy chair. His listlessness and lack of habitual greeting frightened her.

"George, are you all right?"

As if awakened from a reverie George apologized.

"God forgive me my weakness, child. I thought I could give up this land. Maybe I could if it wasn't for the graves. My family lived on and died for this land. I can feel them. I see them coming to me in my dreams and asking me why I failed to let them rest in peace."

Stevie thought for a moment.

"You watch Gigi. I've got a plan."

George smiled as Gigi jumped in his lap and Stevie left quickly and quietly. She walked through the cool night, her boots crunching on gravel.

She reached Ted's house and knocked softly on a decaying panel of the front door. Ted opened the door and stared at her. His red face and bloodshot eyes showed he'd been drinking. She could smell the bourbon on his breath. She steeled herself and said in a confident voice:

"Daddy, we need to talk."

Annoyed and surprised at this nighttime filial assault Ted all but snarled.

"What are you doing here?"

Swallowing all her considerable pride and unshakable belief that it was she who held the moral high ground Stevie softened her tone.

"I know I've been a great disappointment to you."

Here she hesitated. She was hesitating, not for effect but because all her instincts were screaming at her to turn and run and she was debating with herself whether to obey them.

"Can I come in?"

Ted was equally hesitant but in his case it was the copious application of Jim Beam that vitiated his resolve to tell her to go straight to hell. He said,

"I don't know."

Stevie took a few steps inside then walked to Ted's study and was baffled when she noticed the relic case was empty of everything except a well-worn and faded wool Confederate battle flag, which he could not bear to part with as it was the last tangible symbol of all he had once valued and now lost forever, as distant as the way of life it represented.

"Daddy, the guns, the swords . . . they're all gone. Did you sell them all?"

"What difference does it make? I had no one to leave them to."

"Daddy, I never asked you for anything in my life but . . . I need your help." She continued.

"We both have too much pride but I'm asking you to forgive me if not for my sake then for Gigi. She is innocent."

"I don't know what to say."

Stevie drew close enough to her father to almost touch his stubbly, bearded face with her own.

"Daddy, I'm in big trouble. I need $60,000 or George will lose his land and I'll lose Little Souls."

Ted turned away and stared at the opposite blank, peeling plaster wall for a long moment. He turned back and spoke, each word dripping with venom.

"You come to me asking for a father's forgiveness. But what you really want is money to save a man, a nigger no less, that you treat more like a father than you do me. You don't deserve to be inside these Sanders's walls. Get out! Leave my house!"

"I'll lose Little Souls."

This was too much for Ted who was almost ready to use physical violence.

"Get out of my house!"

"Daddy, for once try to understand how I feel. The world's coming down on me right now."

Ted advanced toward her, his right hand raised to strike in the gesture she'd known all too well as a child.

"I said GET OUT!"

Stevie cowered and wailed.

"They're trying to take away my little girl."

Ted took a half step closer hand still raised and Stevie fled out the door. Ted slammed the door so hard a large chunk of decorative plaster fell from the ceiling. He walked quickly to the kitchen, grabbed the fifth of Jim Beam and tilted it and drank, his body shaking with rage and his prominent Adam's apple pulsating as the soothing bourbon flowed down his throat. Stevie wandered toward George's house choking and sobbing, scalding hot tears streaming down her face.

Poor Judgment

The lights were low in Daniel's room, or at least as low and as dim as was possible in such a room. A single, raspberry-scented Yankee candle cast a warm glow on Cheryl's tawny, smooth back as she sat on the edge of the bed fastening her bra. Daniel was admiring her elegant shoulders from his vantage point in the bathroom.

"Don't much like the way those boys at Hunter's were looking at you today."

Daniel emerged delicately scratching his small, well-muscled butt.

Cheryl's face was wreathed in a broad smile, which was reflected in her reply.

"Don't tell me you were jealous. I left simply because I just didn't like the atmosphere all that much."

"Well I've got no grounds to be really, being as we're not exclusive or anything."

Daniel sat heavily in the shabby, cloth-upholstered chair, slow and with the typical masculine content evidenced after heavy sex.

"You women are always trying to stake a claim on a man."

"I'm not trying to stake a claim, Daniel, though it would be nice. Then maybe you'd have the right to get jealous."

"Don't much like being exclusive. It makes a woman change."

"I'm not like any other women you've been with Daniel."

Without thinking through what he was saying, sated as he was with satisfaction of his carnal appetites, Daniel replied,

"Well that's for sure. You being the first black girl I've ever been with."

Cheryl dressed quickly and began to grab her purse and everything she had brought with her.

The bitter disappointment was manifested in her reply.

"I should have known better."

Daniel sat up, ice filling his body where seconds ago there had been nothing but warmth.

"Now wait, hold on. I didn't mean it like that."

Cheryl seized her car keys and practically flew to the door and threw it open.

"Please, Daniel, don't even try to explain."

She shut the door hard leaving Daniel to contemplate the ruins of what had been a really great evening.

"Damnit! You stupid, stupid ass!"

Stevie was still crying when she reached George's door and knocked. He opened it immediately. She burst out:

"I'm so sorry, George. I failed you."

George took her in a fierce embrace and she dampened his right shoulder with her tears.

"That's all right, child," he said softly and his deep bass voice comforted her.

"This is no time to give up. There's too much at stake. We got to get ourselves ready for court tomorrow."

Pastor Peter awakened with a start. He reached for the well-carved magnolia wood crucifix over his headboard, a seminary graduation gift from his father. He wiped some night sweat from his face and took several deep breaths to slow his pounding heart. He rose from the bed, went to the door and walked slowly out into the darkness, which enveloped him.

CHAPTER 29

A Temporary Relapse

Hunter's Bar was in the process of closing for the night or rather the early morning. The last patrons were weaving their unsteady way out the door. Some to return to their likely to be angry partners and others to a lonely room. Duncan shut the door behind the final departing tippler with a sigh of relief. Only one soul remained seated on a stool at the bar behind a forest of empty Budweiser bottles and almost as many glass tumblers. Daniel was very drunk and Duncan admired the fact that he hadn't yet fallen off the stool. He was quietly mumbling to himself rather incoherently.

"Sons a bitches. Tell me . . . I'm the one . . . I know what I did . . ."

Duncan walked up behind him and Daniel twisted around using his right hand on one of the legs of the stool as an aid to remaining upright.

"Hey . . . my man . . . I need another one of these . . . these things here."

Duncan watched Daniel pointing to one of the Buds.

"No more, Daniel. Gotta close."

Daniel was incredulous and frustrated.

"Hey! No more nothing . . . I'm not done."

"Yeah you are."

"No listen, I got things, problems to sort out. You can't cut me off."

Duncan shook his head and began to walk off.

"Yeah, you got problems all right, you keep laying down with that nigger."

Daniel lurched off the stool, in process he knocked over bottles, glasses, some of which crashed to the floor and broke. He went for Duncan.

"Don'! Don you don' talk about her like that."

Duncan grabbed Daniel and wrestled him to the floor with little effort. Daniel burped and the smell made Duncan gag. Daniel belched out:

"You stupid redneck."

Duncan lifted Daniel like a rag doll and slammed him down into the nearest wooden chair and held him there to keep Daniel from tipping the chair over. Duncan said with both exasperation and a modicum of tolerance in his tone:

"I'm a stupid redneck? What the hell are you then? Deputy drunk?"

Duncan left him and went for the phone by the bar all the while Daniel was in danger of falling out of the chair babbling more or less coherently.

"Call my girl that."

"Your 'girl'?"

Duncan dialed.

"Sheriff, sorry it's late but you gotta come get Daniel. No, it's worse. Okay."

He hung up and waited.

Pastor Peter shuffled back into the church proper. With heavy footsteps he walked slowly to the worn oak pew in the very front, then dropped to his knees, hands resting on the back and began to pray.

The sheriff arrived at Hunter's much to Duncan's relief. Wordlessly Duncan pointed to Daniel who was slumped over the chair still mumbling one moment and sobbing the next. The sheriff looked down at his son.

"Okay, son. Time to go home."

Daniel raised his head with some difficulty, recognized his father, then spoke with slurred words.

"I ain' going nowhere . . . I don' wanna go nowhere . . ."

The sheriff pushed his hands under Daniel's armpits and began to lift him.

"Let's go."

Daniel resisted and protested.

"No! I don't wanna."

The sheriff, who was a powerful man proceeded to drag Daniel out of the bar, wrestled him into the patrol vehicle and drove off. When they arrived at Daniel's room, Daniel was slightly more sober and he walked in of his own accord. He turned to face his father.

"Don't ya see, Dad? Don't you see, I'm a goddamned loser? I ruin everything."

The sheriff looked hard into Daniel's bloodshot, puffy, and swollen eyes. He spoke with conviction.

"No, you're not, son."

The sheriff tried to get Daniel to the bed but he broke away from his father's embrace.

"Stop covering for me. I am. Everything's my fault and he's gone."

He continued though he was emotionally shattered.

"I've messed up every relationship I ever had. Luke's gone and I miss him. And I just keep spoiling one thing after another."

The sheriff walked out without a word and in a very few minutes returned with a beige manila envelope.

"Maybe it's time you see this. I don't know what it says, but good, bad or indifferent it may put a stop to this bullshit of yours one way or the other. Luke left this next to his badge. I've been afraid to let you read it. It's really none of my business anyway."

The envelope was marked in large black ink in Luke's script: "FOR DANIEL."

Daniel took the letter from the envelope and began to read.

"Daniel, I love you bro. I forgive you for whatever you think you did to me. She never was any good for either of us. I just can't take this life anymore. It's got nothing to do with you, I promise. I love you. I always have."

It was signed "Luke."

Daniel dropped the letter on the bed and covering his face with both hands began to cry so hard his entire body shook.

Cheryl had stopped her car by the roadside less than a mile from Daniel's place. She was unnerved by the sudden hard right turn in their relationship. Was he just another white man who could not see her as an attractive woman but as an attractive black woman, some exotic musky scented, forbidden creature, with whom to experience some to his mind, sick, sordid sort of sex and then race back to a woman of his own skin color and white cultural upbringing? Then again Daniel had seemed to transcend Southern stereotypes. He was clearly sensitive. Then why had he spoken like every other white male asshole she knew other than the sheriff, whose redneck qualities were at least honest and upfront. Daniel had totally blindsided her. Then again maybe he had simply misspoken and meant nothing by it. Listening to a dreamy song by Lana Del Rey, tears wet on her cheeks, Cheryl stared into the night, wondering.

Ted Sanders sat hunched over a clean sheet of white paper near the fireplace in his study. The burning pine logs lit the paper with a flickering but strong light. Using a ballpoint pen he wrote. "Dear Stephanie: You asked me to forgive you." He set down the pen and his face contorted with momentary disgust. He impulsively seized the paper, tore it in two, crumpled the pieces, and fed them to the flames where they first browned then caught fire and burned, curling into ash. He opened the Bible and paged to Psalm 46: "God is in the midst of her; she shall not be moved." Frustrated he stood allowing the Bible to fall to the floor. He wandered aimlessly out of the room past the fire.

CHAPTER 30

A Day in Court

Stevie had taken unusual pains to dress both herself and Gigi in order to appear conventionally respectable for their day in court. This took some doing given their habitually casual approach to their daily clothing. Unaccustomed to having her long hair in anything but a carefree flowing style, Gigi rebelled and refused to put on her dress until Stevie agreed to braid it; which was reserved for truly special occasions and posed a trial to her mother as Stevie was not very skilled at plaiting Gigi's hair. At the courthouse with its marble steps and Doric façade, the most impressive building in the county, built during the Great Depression, standing beside George and Gigi, Stevie paused, looked at her watch then the three of them trooped in.

The courtroom had white plaster walls with some mahogany trim and an oil portrait of the judge on one wall. The bench was raised above the rest of the court. A brass nameplate stood on the bench reading Judge Nathan Stein. Judge Stein was a fit, fifty-something secular Jew, with a deserved reputation as a legal scholar, one which was somewhat leavened by a marked streak of eccentricity in some of his decisions. Stevie, Gigi, and George were seated in the front chairs facing the judge's bench as Angel Wells from Children's Services took the witness stand and was sworn in by the bailiff. She was dressed in a dark blue skirt and starched white blouse. Her hair was coiled in its usual tight bun. Mason Parks, wearing his favorite Saville Row suit sat in the very back, unknown to Stevie and George; though Judge Stein knew him or at least of him and wondered why one of the most powerful, perceptive, and dangerous barristers in Tennessee would bother to drive hours to Zion to witness a legal proceeding as devoid of legal significance as a parental fitness hearing involving such unknown individuals. He was suspicious to say the least. Judge Stein shrugged and looked at the pictures the investigator had taken as she began addressing him.

"Your Honor, the yard was unbelievable. I have never seen so much filth. I even stepped in some."

Judge Stein raised his bushy eyebrows.

"Ms. Wells, who took these pictures?"

"I don't know. They just appeared on my desk in an envelope."

At this admission the judge rolled his eyes heavenward. He said with a strong hint of sarcasm in his tone:

"I particularly like the child's sneaker buried in the dog poop. Nice touch."

Ignoring the judge's apparent skepticism in regard to the graphic images, Angel continued in a voice redolent with suppressed outrage.

"My subsequent investigations prove that Ms. Sanders leads a highly abnormal, even aberrant lifestyle."

Mason Parks could see that Ms. Wells's testimony was not only not favorably impressing the judge, but also, in fact, her indignation was having the opposite effect. She was a rank amateur at assessing this particular judge and was undoubtedly used to having her assessments rubber-stamped by bored jurists. He smiled at her mystification. He could almost hear her thoughts: "Why isn't he believing me?" He said to himself: "Busybody buffoon." Judge Stein replied with two somewhat scornfully spoken words.

"Do tell."

Not to be put off by the judge's palpable disdain, Angel dutifully soldiered on.

"She drives around at all hours picking up dead and injured animals. She and Mr. Jackson," here she pointed at George. Implied but missing from the Mr. Jackson comment was "a Negro."

"Operate Little Souls Cemetery. She's an alternative veterinarian."

The implied "Negro" was not lost on the judge and disdain was rapidly morphing into scorn. The judge made a steeple of his fingers and looked closely at Angel.

"Exactly how do these ah, aberrations, as you refer to them, constitute a danger to the child?"

Angel spoke with the first hint of irritation in her tone.

"The child is a frequent passenger on these excursions. Everything about Ms. Sanders is irregular."

The judge took a Q-tip from the right pocket of his black robe and began to clean his right ear. At this gesture, Mason Parks had difficulty repressing a guffaw. Clearly Ms. Wells was failing to gain any traction with her testimony. Puzzled she said,

"Can you hear me, Your Honor?"

Judge Stein continued to twirl the Q-tip then looked at the large, white-faced clock on the wall. He smiled at Angel.

"Please continue."

"The filth in Ms. Sanders's yard is in an area where her child plays. This alone is sufficient cause for removal."

George was holding Gigi, who was by now bored by the entire judicial proceeding and fidgeted but otherwise had remained unusually quiet.

"Are you suggesting the filth be removed? I could simply order her to clean it up. Surely you are not placing a child in the same category as the removal of a dumpster?"

Sensing that the Child Services woman was getting nowhere with the judge Stevie decided it was time to be heard. Her tone was more confident than she felt.

"Your Honor, may I speak?"

Judge Stein looked down over his glasses to Angel.

"Ms. Wells?"

Relieved to be off the stand and away from the judge's sallies, she agreed.

"I'm finished, Your Honor."

The judge looked with a faint smile at Stevie.

"Ms. Sanders, I would remind you that you're under oath."

Daniel Olsen entered the courtroom in full, freshly pressed uniform, his hat on straight. Though there were dark circles under his puffy eyes, they were otherwise clear and he looked every inch like a textbook deputy sheriff. He took a seat two rows behind Stevie. Stevie began.

"Your Honor, I know I have a lot of animals but I keep my place clean. I don't know who took those pictures but that one with the shoe is faked. I came home and found all this."

The judge ran his fingers through his still thick, black, and glossy hair, which he wore past his ears.

"I assume I've heard testimony from everyone concerned with this case."

Daniel stood, resplendent in his uniform. His tone radiated authority.

"No, Your Honor."

"And you are?"

"Deputy sheriff, Daniel Olsen."

Judge Stein smiled with genuine warmth.

"I know your father."

"I'd like to state for the record that Stephanie Sanders is an exemplary parent. I've known her for over twenty years."

Mason Parks stood, handsome and urbane in his suit, but somewhat out of place in the Zion County court.

"May I address the court?"

Unruffled by the appearance of the famed Nashville attorney, the judge questioned him, though he knew Parks identity, and was somewhat in awe of his reputation.

"And you are?"

Observing all the expected formalities as if he were in Washington trying a case before the United States Supreme Court, which he had done more than once, he approached the bench and handed his card to the bailiff who passed it on to the judge.

Judge Stein studied the white parchment with the raised black lettering then looked at Mason and said with only the faintest hint of irony in his voice.

"And to what do we provincials owe the honor of your presence?"

"I represent Theodore Sanders, the child's maternal grandfather."

He paused for effect then continued.

"Of course there is no paternal grandfather or any father of record for that matter."

"And where is Theodore Sanders?"

"He is at home, Your Honor. He prays the court to award custody of Gabriella Sanders to him."

The judge was annoyed.

"Mr. Parks, are you aware that this is only a fitness and not a custody hearing?"

"My client only wished the court to know there is an alternative to Child Services."

At this Judge Stein looked fixedly at Stevie but spoke to Mason.

"Isn't Mr. Sanders the gentleman with the rather large Confederate flag out on County Hollow Road?"

Mason could see that his position was in peril.

"Mr. Sanders is a very sentimental gentleman of the old school, Your Honor."

The judge gazed panoramically around the courtroom.

"Let's see. We have a choice between an abundance of feces, Children's Services, or Jefferson Davis. Not much of a choice here is there?"

The judge paused, then delivered his decision.

"I'm going to continue this matter for thirty days. Ms. Wells, you will categorize and weigh all the feces present on the Sanders property each day for the next thirty and file a daily report with the court."

Angel Wells could hardly believe her ears. Utterly dumbfounded, she blurted,

"What the?"

She bit off the hell but she really wanted to say fuck.

Judge Stein favored Angel with a rather cruel smile. He thought that the employment of her and Children's Services might be a ploy by Mason Parks, for otherwise why was such an eminent barrister involved with this unimportant hearing to begin with. He rapped his gavel sharply.

"Court stands in recess."

Cheryl was driving to the sheriff's office, still unnerved by Daniel's behavior and low-class, racist comment coming after they had such great

sex and shared intimate, loving banter. She failed to see a sharp-edged, deep pothole in the macadam, which popped her right front tire like a birthday balloon. She called the wrecking service and in less than fifteen minutes she saw the flashing yellow light bar of the H&B wrecker. Bill sat in the passenger seat looking back, using the side mirror as Hank filled out a service order and handed it to Cheryl. The animosity they had displayed the other day at Hunter's was washed away by the prospect of taking her money, which they were badly in need of despite Ted's largess, mostly due to the considerable bar tabs both men kept at Hunter's. Hank spoke in a businesslike tone.

"Sign that and we'll get a start on that tire."

Cheryl signed the work order.

"Do I get a copy?"

"Sure."

Hank gave Cheryl the yellow copy. She took it and stared at the handwriting. She remembered seeing that childish block printing somewhere.

CHAPTER 31

An Afternoon
at Judge Stein's

Mason Parks drove his prized, blue Porsche 356 B Super 90 cabriolet convertible very slowly down the gravel driveway so as to avoid any possible paint chips. He came to a stop in the circle just in front of the columned, white-painted Georgian home. As he shut down the engine a lovely twentyish woman with flaming red hair came up and admired the Porsche.

"Hi. I'm Elizabeth can I help you? This is a really beautiful old car."

Mason was thinking:

"And you are a really beautiful girl."

He would have taken time to banter with Elizabeth as he liked pretty women but he was there on business and wanted to get back to Nashville and Jocelyn.

"I'm looking for the judge."

Elizabeth laughed.

"He's out back swimming."

"In this weather?"

The temperature was in the fifties.

She laughed again, a full, throaty, joyous laugh that intrigued Mason. She pointed to the rear of the house.

"You'll find him through the trees."

Mason was tempted to ask her who and what she was exactly in relation to the judge but prudence prevailed and he contented himself with a sincere.

"Thank you, Elizabeth."

He watched her disappear back into the house and he walked some distance through the trees down to a large pond ringed with lush grass which a fine paint horse was busy cropping with enthusiasm, so much so he barely raised his shapely head as Mason approached. Seeing Mason, the judge swam to shore using compact overhead strokes and in minutes he emerged dripping and naked whereupon he donned a thick, fleecy long robe, which he secured with a cloth belt. He looked at Mason with genuine surprise.

"I don't recall inviting you, but now that you are here would you care for a swim?"

Unwilling to rebuff the judge's hospitality but being averse to swimming in ponds in general for fear of waterborne flesh-eating bacteria, necrotizing faciitis, and cold plunges of any variety, Mason put his right hand gingerly in the water being careful to step on solid ground to avoid muddying his rather costly brown Oxfords. The water was icy from a week of rather chilly nights.

"Thank you but no."

He spoke deferentially.

"I came to ask you to reconsider your decision in the Gabriella Sanders case."

Judge Stein looked at Mason and there was no mistaking his attitude from his tone, which was nearly as icy as the pond water.

"Mr. Parks, a young girl needs her mother."

Judge Stein was about to waggle his locally notorious index finger at the attorney but as Mason Parks was known in the highest Tennessee legal circles as a man to be reckoned with, he decided that discretion was the better part of valor. He continued.

"If you think a little or even a lot of dog . . ."

He was about to use the term he had employed in court as Gabriella was in the room but here he had no need for such niceties. The judge said,

"shit would convince me otherwise you're sadly mistaken."

Taking off the gloves so to speak, Parks shot back.

"But she needs a father as well."

Losing patience, Judge Stein said sarcastically:

"Fine. If you can find the father, do the child a favor and remind him of his paternal obligations."

At his wits' end Mason made a last ditch attempt to salvage what was otherwise looking like a long drive, a wasted day, and a lot of unnecessary miles on his beloved Porsche, though he did enjoy driving it more than his Jaguar F type, which he thought was both overrated and overpriced. He was thinking of trading it in on an Audi A8.

"My client is willing to assume that role." From the pained look on Stein's face Mason knew he had made an error. The judge's voice positively dripped with scorn as he replied,

"Do you really think a grandfather who hoists a huge stars-and-bars flag every day is a desirable guardian? You cannot be serious."

Mason Parks knew he was being dismissed and leaving empty-handed.

"Now if you'll excuse me, my hot bath is waiting."

Back in his Porsche, Mason was only slightly irritated by the day's events. His approach to life's inevitable setbacks followed a simple principle. Never get mad, get even, or rather, get as far ahead of even as possible. As he looked at the Porsche's odometer he smiled to himself and said under his breath:

"Ted Sanders, you owe me three hundred dollars a mile."

Duncan Hunter was putting clean, heavy, green glass ashtrays on tables when he heard a car drive up. It was early afternoon and there were no patrons in the bar. The door swung open and Cheryl walked in, much to the owner's surprise. Duncan was not such a bigot that he failed to appreciate that Cheryl was one very good looking woman, in spite of what he thought of her skin color.

"Afternoon," she said in a matter of fact voice. Duncan replied politely.

"What can I do for you?"

"I was heading back to the station but I thought I'd stop in to let you know that we know who tossed the rocks through your windows."

Duncan put down the ashtray he was wiping with a terry cloth and was all attention. Hunter's Bar was his one passion in life and he viewed the attack on his windows as an assault on his very being. Cheryl approached and spread the note reading "Hunting is Murder" that had been wrapped around one of the rocks that had shattered his window on the table. She then carefully unfolded the H&B work order and placed it beside the other. Duncan stared at the printing and though he was prejudiced due to his upbringing, he was anything but stupid. His eyes narrowed and his face flushed. He looked up from the notes and smiled at Cheryl. He said very politely and respectfully.

"Young lady, can I buy you a cup of coffee?"

CHAPTER 32

Changes
and Challenges

Sheriff Olsen pulled up and parked in front of the Sanders mansion. He stepped carefully up the porch stairs avoiding putting too much weight on the second stair, which was partially rotted. He knocked on the front door using the large, bronze knocker but there was no response from inside. He took his lead sap from his pant's pocket and rapped smartly. After several minutes a disheveled and bearded Ted opened the door and left it open as the sheriff followed Ted into the den.

"Word is that you're after custody of your granddaughter. Ted?"

Ted said nothing and didn't even look at the sheriff. Olsen shrugged and without being invited sat down in Ted's armchair. He looked at the

gun cabinet, empty except for an old Damascus barrel hammer shotgun of dubious manufacture.

"Looks like we won't be target practicing with your old Winchester a whole lot anymore."

Ted turned to face the sheriff and seeing him occupying the only chair in the den, sat down on the old hook rug by the fire. He replied in a lifeless, flat tone devoid of any affect:

"Suppose not."

The sheriff was concerned. He'd seen this sort of behavior in men and women on the verge of suicide.

"Ted. I said, Ted, are you all right? Last time I remember seeing anyone sit like you are was in that photo of a Buddhist monk who poured gasoline all over and set himself on fire. Protesting the war."

Ted, who had been staring at his naked and not too clean, long-nailed feet, looked up slowly and spoke in a monotone.

"Which war?"

Daniel's patrol vehicle was parked on the side of the road. To say he was anxious would be an understatement. He was sitting on the edge of his seat as he flipped the toggle on the police radio. After he did so, he nervously rubbed a small object between the fingers of his right hand. His voice was tentative. He began.

"Hey, it's Daniel."

Cheryl was in the station monitoring the radio though Daniel was the only active patrol. She heard the quaver in his voice but she was determined to say nothing until he finished making his case for her forgiveness then she would either convict and forget him or acquit him and continue the relationship.

"I, uh, just want you to know that, well things have been real hard for me for a while. I've done some very stupid things, and uh, well I really like you, and I don't care what anyone thinks or says. It's time people around here grow up a little, and you, you are just so pretty, and you treat me like, like well like I'm worth something and no one's really done that before and I like being with you . . ."

He kept fondling the small gold-and-diamond heart pendant on a delicately chased gold chain until he felt the chain was becoming tangled. He drew a deep breath and continued.

"So I got you something, I hope you like it, but maybe it can mean that uh, well that you're my girl, and we can just see what happens from there. I'm gonna stop drinking so much, cause, uh, cause my brother see, he actually didn't blame me for what happened."

Daniel was overcome by the memory of Luke's deathbed note and his mouth was so dry his voice cracked like an adolescent in puberty. He swallowed and cleared his throat.

"And you never judged me when I thought differently."

Cheryl had listened to the whole apologia with critical interest, assessing the degree of introspection and soul searching behind Daniel's words. Had he made one misstep however minor, much less a major blunder similar to the one that had engendered her flight from his room, she would have permanently erased him from her personal life and written him off entirely. His combination apology, confession, and most important his profession of affection had moved her and the icy, sick feeling in her abdomen melted and she wanted to be with him. Her voice was warm and inviting as she spoke.

"Daniel Olsen. How soon can I see you?"

Daniel heaved a mighty sigh of blessed relief knowing he was forgiven and any sort of forgiveness was worth more to his tortured soul than words could have expressed. He switched off the radio and began humming Steve Winwood's, "Back in the High Life."

Hank and Bill were driving in their wrecker out on the road near the charred remains of Stevie's tent, which the local authorities seemed to be in no hurry to remove. Bill was smoking a Swisher as he had only a very limited supply of the better cigars as Hank drove. The afternoon was advancing and Tim McGraw's "Redneck Girl" was playing loud on the truck radio. As they passed the ruined tent they high-fived each other, laughing uproariously. They were turning into the gravel parking lot of Hunter's when Hank noticed the sheriff's SUV with the light bar flashing. He nudged Bill who turned and saw the lights.

"What the hell?"

Hank stopped just inside the parking lot and killed the engine. Sheriff Olsen exited the SUV and walked up to the wrecker. Hank said politely:

"Afternoon, Sheriff. I wasn't speeding or anything like that was I?"

The sheriff smiled.

"No, you weren't. You boys get out of the truck now and don't give me a hard time."

"So what's the problem?"

The sheriff produced two sets of handcuffs.

"You're both under arrest."

"What the hell is going on? We haven't done anything."

Bill nudged Hank as the sheriff told them their rights under the Miranda ruling.

"You've got to be fooling," said Hank.

Sheriff Olsen held out the handcuffs.

"Now you boys can either put those on or make me do it."

Hank and Bill were incredulous but as they were still relatively sober both decided to cooperate. The sheriff's tone left no doubt that he was serious.

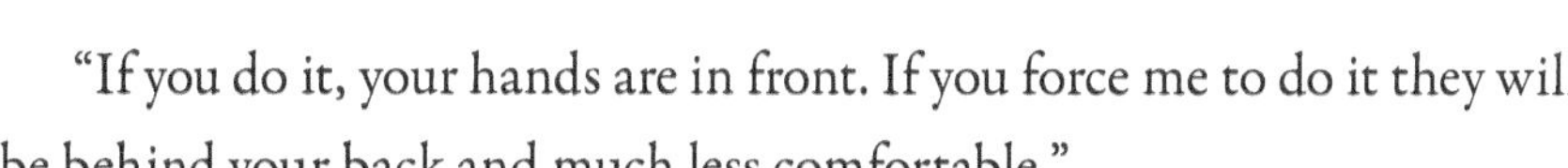

"If you do it, your hands are in front. If you force me to do it they will be behind your back and much less comfortable."

Hank was the first to obey instructions. He cuffed himself and stood quietly. Bill threw down his cigar in disgust and very reluctantly cuffed himself.

The sheriff opened the back doors to the SUV and motioned to Hank and Bill who got in and sat while the sheriff closed both doors. He drove off, red lights flashing.

Stevie was brushing down her black-and-white rescue quarter horse when an unfamiliar van pulled up. She felt the hairs on the back of her neck stand up expecting an attack. Then she saw the van was somewhat familiar and she relaxed. Sam exited looking forlorn and disheveled. Stevie dropped the brush, ran over, and hugged him hard. In a quavering voice Sam spoke.

"She didn't make it."

"Oh, Sam. I'm so sorry."

Stevie broke off the embrace and looked at Sam for a long moment. He sounded stronger now.

"I want her to rest here at Little Souls."

She nodded and Sam opened the rear gates of the van. Stevie leaned down, gathered up, and then reverently cradled Brandy in her arms.

Later that day, Sam, George, and Stevie were standing beside a fresh grave as George intoned a blessing with reverence in his deep bass voice.

"And Lord, bless Brandy, beloved companion and friend of Sam Williams and Sam's father Harold Williams."

Sam looked up at Stevie who nodded. Sam leaned down holding Brandy's worn leather collar and placed it gently on the mounded earth at the head of the grave. Stevie shoveled the remaining dirt over the collar as George continued the service.

"We know Brandy's in a better place and we ask you Lord to let her join with Harold now and with Sam Williams someday when he, too, enters Your Kingdom. Amen."

Stevie and Sam echoed George with a heartfelt:

"Amen."

Stevie and Sam watched as George tapped a white painted cross into the ground with a wooden mallet.

Bad News for Ted

Mason Parks was examining the rocker panels of his Porsche for any damage from the gravel and weeds in Ted's dilapidated driveway. It was not easy in the fading light. Satisfied that no serious harm was done he gingerly walked up the steps to the front door and eschewing the bronze knocker as possibly unclean he banged on the door with his palm. Ted answered unusually quickly as he was expecting the attorney. The two men did not shake hands and went inside to the den. Mason looked disapprovingly at the mangled eagle, its missing wing and tail feathers, and the odd angle of the mount resulting from a missing foot. Ted spoke first.

"Well, how did it go?"

Mason faced him with a blank look thinking that the eagle was not the only occupant of the den that looked disheveled and forlorn. Then he smiled thinly.

"Unfortunately, Judge Stein took a rather dim view of your flag. You might consider removing the stars and bars in favor of the stars and stripes."

Ted sneered.

"Typical left-wing sheeny, Jew kike. So what do we do now?"

Mason made a steeple of his fingers as he contemplated just how much to punish Ted for sending him on a fool's errand to Zion and the subsequent wear and tear on the Porsche.

"That all depends."

"Depends on what?"

Mason said in a silky voice, the one he used when playing to a jury.

"On whether you can raise another $20,000."

Ted exploded.

"But I've already paid you for everything!"

Mason was unruffled by the outburst. He replied in an even tone.

"You paid for everything we have executed on your behalf thus far. If you wish to pursue custody of your granddaughter beyond the hearing that was just held before Judge Stein, we will be entering a new phase and additional expense."

The mention of more money and a new phase emptied Ted of bluster and he began to whine plaintively.

"I've sold all my heirlooms, even my guns. You hold my mortgage. I've nothing left to my name."

He looked at Mason with tears springing from his bloodshot, veined, watery eyes.

"I've lost it all, my wife, my daughter, my granddaughter. Now I'll lose Sanders Plantation."

Mason had decided even before he paid this visit to Ted that the repulsive old man's money was far less attractive than the prospect of humiliating and hopefully completing his destruction. Ted had insulted Jocelyn not that she cared, and him, wasted his time, and in trying to harm his daughter would doubtless cause irreparable harm to an innocent child. Mason was not an inherently evil man. He was, indeed, tough but he was ethical in his own quixotic way and Ted had grievously offended his eccentric sense of fair play. If it were not for Mason's father's relationship with Ted's father he would have no more agreed to see him to begin with than he would have entertained an Eastern diamondback rattlesnake on his Chippendale partner's desk. He felt soiled by having had anything to do with Ted and his maniacal quest for vengeance on Stephanie. Mason wanted to cleanse and free himself from having any relations with Ted by cutting all ties, and if it cost money so be it. He took some papers from his inside jacket pocket and tossed them on the table in front of Ted.

"Here's the paperwork on your property. You can have it back. I can't find anything of value to me in this land. It's contaminated by your very presence."

Ted was speechless. Mason leaned toward him and looked Ted straight in his damp eyes.

"I'll be leaving now, Mr. Sanders. But before I do I'll share a thought with you, free of charge. You are a disgrace to the South and to the United States of America. Frankly speaking, you, your actions, and your very existence are utterly disgusting to me."

Completely taken aback and dumbfounded by Mason's denunciation, Ted stood stock-still and stared at the elegant attorney. Mason opened his black leather briefcase and removing a manila folder handed it to Ted who took it with a quivering and nerveless right hand.

"You might as well have these. You paid for them."

Without a further word or backward glance, Mason snapped his briefcase shut, turned on his heels and stalked out of the room. Holding the folder as if it were some sort of protective talisman, Ted heard the Porsche's motor

rumble to life and the exhaust sound slowly fade as it rolled down the driveway. He sat down in his chair and opened the folder. It contained a number of 8" x 10" color, glossy photographs of Stevie, Gigi, and Pastor Peter taken throughout the past week. There were a few of Stevie and the pastor being rather more demonstrative in their relations than is customary between a parishioner and her pastor, but nothing that would definitively stamp the embraces and kisses on cheek as illicit even in Ted's intolerant view. The last photo was of Pastor Peter and Stevie locked in the undeniable, sexually charged, passionate kiss following Stevie's baptism. Ted dropped the folder as if it burned his fingers and the photos fell on the floor. He walked to a small, fragile, walnut nightstand with a single drawer. He opened it and took out the old "pencil barrel" Colt .22 Woodsman, the same one with which he had killed the injured raccoon when Stevie was a child.

CHAPTER 34

Confrontations

Stevie looked out her bedroom window in the trailer and saw the lights in George's house go out. She went to Gigi's small but imaginatively furnished bedroom and tucked her in. Just then her phone trilled.

"Hello?"

Daniel was calling from his room.

"Sorry to call so late."

"That's okay, Daniel. What is it?"

"I had a call from Mason Parks, the fancy Nashville attorney your father hired to steal Gigi. It turns out that Ted had paid him to take over George's mortgage. I thought it was important you should know right away."

As Stevie was taking in this shocking information Daniel continued.

"And the sheriff was at your dad's house today. He looked at your father's old stuffed eagle. It was missing a lot of feathers and the right

talon. Stevie, your dad was framing you with the Feds. And he even hired those two wrecker drivers to throw rocks at Hunter's Bar, burn your tent, everything. Dad arrested them this afternoon at Hunter's. They are in jail and confessing everything."

Stevie was about to faint but then her shock soon changed to anger.

"Oh my God . . ."

"I'm so sorry but I thought you needed to know. We'll have to pick him up in the morning."

Daniel paused then continued.

"And he will likely be facing some Federal charges."

Stevie put the phone down and tried to slow her racing heart with deep breaths.

"Stevie?"

Hearing nothing, Daniel hung up and clicked off the bedside lamp. Cheryl lay sound asleep, the gold pendant glinting in the moonlight between her breasts. Daniel smiled at the sight then curled up next to her.

Pastor Peter was in his bedroom at the rear of the church standing in his white boxers sipping a glass of pinot noir and contemplating his ministerial garments that were hanging in the compact closet. He walked somewhat unsteadily to the unfinished pine dresser and studied his face in the bright, steel-framed mirror. He was less than happy to see bags under his brown eyes and the beginning of crow's feet at the corners. He was more satisfied with the musculature of his chest and his flat abdomen. His gaze dropped from the mirror to the gold-framed photograph on the dresser. It depicted him in civilian dress with Stevie and Gigi. They looked like a happy family. He had always treasured the image and the memory, yet it galled him that Gigi was still unaware that he was not just her spiritual father but her earthly father as well. He picked up the photo and laid it flat atop his large, white buckram-covered Bible with the gilt-stamped lettering. Then he poured the remains of the bottle of pinot into his thin crystal glass goblet topping it up. He brought the glass to his lips and before he could take a sip he heard a sudden and insistent knock at the front door. Startled, Peter hurriedly donned the black ministerial robe and answered the door. Seeing Ted, Peter picked up the wine glass to place it in an inconspicuous place but Ted barged in and forestalled his attempt to conceal his late-night tippling.

"Mr. Sanders. Uh, Ted. This is a surprise."

Peter could smell the overpowering odor of whiskey emanating not only from Ted's breath, but also his entire body, as if he were bathed in bourbon.

"You've been drinking. I can smell it on your breath. You really should go home."

Peter failed to see the irony in his statement given that he was holding a full glass of wine in his hand and was less than sober himself. Ted was too drunk and full of rage to take notice of Peter's rather egregious hypocrisy in regard to his own inebriation.

Ted rounded on Peter and as he did so he held up the photo of Peter and Stevie locked together as only passionate lovers do in his left hand in mute accusation of what he regarded as an unspeakable betrayal. In his right he held the Colt Woodsman. Ted screamed at the top of his lungs.

"Viper! Seducer! Rapist! False Prophet!"

Though completely terrified, mostly of the pistol, the shock of Ted's verbal assault failed to stupefy Peter. He had been unconsciously expecting some similarly dramatic denouement between them for years and now it had come, so he was able to reply albeit in a totally unconvincing squeaky voice.

"What in heaven's name are you talking about?"

Peter desperately wanted to distract Ted and equally importantly, calm himself by setting down the wine glass but as he lowered it, Ted swiped at it viciously with the pistol, shattering it and scattering wine and glass. The stem pierced Peter's palm and driven by the force of the pistol barrel,

buried itself deeply in the ball of his thumb almost through the hand and blood began to well. Peter's falsetto denial only served to add fuel to Ted's burning rage. He spoke in a stentorian tone that would have done credit to the biblical Jeremiah had the prophet been drinking heavily as the words were slurred.

"You know damn well what I'm talking about. You've witnessed my struggles and all the time you were ridiculing me. You and the whole damned town have been laughing and mocking me behind my back for the past five years."

Ted raised the pistol and pointed it directly at Peter's chest at which point the pastor cowered. Then Peter looked down at the largest section of the wine glass's stem protruding from his palm and the continuous upwelling of his blood. He stared at his hand in disbelief. He looked at Ted and held it out to him as if his blood would expiate his guilt. Peter said in a tone of absolute wonderment, as if he had never seen his own blood:

"I'm . . . I'm bleeding."

Ted was much too drunk and far too angry to pay any attention to Peter's wound. Ted's right hand began to shake and he raised the pistol to Peter's forehead. The two men were less than five feet apart. Ted continued to excoriate the pastor.

"I trusted you. You were the one person in the world I thought I could confide in. And you . . . you seduced my only child and ruined my family. You looked me in the eye when I was in anguish, mocking me the whole time. You deserve to die."

Though in such mortal terror that Peter actually wet himself, he could not deny the justice of Ted's accusations; though to be fair he believed he had always been sincere and truthful when he had acted as Ted's spiritual advisor. The untenable and highly irregular situation was due almost entirely to Stevie's dogged insistence on keeping both the affair and Gigi's birth secret from Ted and the world. Peter bowed his head, waiting for the report of the pistol. Then from some inner recess of his being, from a primal instinct to survive, he spoke.

"I'm so sorry. I love Stephanie. She absolutely refused to marry me. It's not my fault."

Peter held his wrist tight to serve as a tourniquet in order to staunch the increasing flow of blood, which began to form a widening dark puddle on the hardwood floor. Ted lowered the pistol for a moment then raised it again.

"It's your fault. She came to you for guidance. But you, you led her down the path of disobedience, disgrace, and destruction."

Though horrified not so much by his previous actions or even Ted's justified accusations, as by the amount of blood he imagined he was losing, he was beginning to feel he might just survive the encounter. His voice was quavering but stronger.

"I've done you a terrible wrong. I ask you in God's holy name to forgive me."

Peter's invoking the name of God, the Old Testament "Vengeance is mine sayeth the Lord" sort of deity that Ted favored over the meeker, milder, friendlier, forgiving God, not only failed to mollify him but also angered him even more if such a thing were possible. Now Ted wanted to utterly humiliate, devastate, and shame his former pastor, exactly as to his mind, the pastor had shamed and humiliated him by seducing and impregnating his daughter far outside the bounds of holy matrimony.

"You dare call on God's holy name? You who have have betrayed Him and everything your ministry stands for!"

Ted watched the pastor whose head he thought was bowed in the shame he so richly deserved. He thundered in a tone that Moses might have used to address the followers of Dathan.

"Now confess! Tell me!!!! Tell me everything you did to Stephanie!"

Peter began to pray fervently and by doing so he transformed himself into the pastor that had been Ted's spiritual rock and not the seducer Ted so despised that he was about to murder him.

"The Lord is my shepherd. I shall not want. He maketh me to lie down in green pastures. He leadeth me beside the still waters. He restoreth my soul. Yea though I walk through the valley of the shadow of death . . ."

Watching the pastor, head bowed, as meek as a lamb to the slaughter failed to move Ted from his need to humiliate the man. He shouted,

"Tell me the name of the man who bastardized my granddaughter!"

Thinking that at any moment a bullet would enter his brain, Peter cried out in terror hoping his long history and sincere acceptance of responsibility might just save him.

"It was I. I am the one . . ."

Ted pushed the muzzle of the .22 against Peter's forehead. He moved his index finger from the front grip strap of the pistol and onto the grooved trigger. He was ready to squeeze when Peter burst out,

"But she always said whenever I asked, even begged her, on my knees to be my lawfully wedded wife, that she could never marry me because I reminded her too much of you!"

This had an instantaneous, dramatic, and sobering effect on Ted. He had been so fixated on revenge that his previous actions had been automatic, reducing him to a human automaton as if he were in a fugue state. Peter's outburst had penetrated his all-consuming mania with an illuminating beam of realization, as effective as God's had been on Saul when he was on his way to Damascus to persecute more Christians. Ted looked at the gun in his hand as if he'd never seen it before, then he threw it against the wall where it discharged. The bullet struck the wood figure of Christ above Peter's bed piercing the image's right calf. Ted wheeled and fled out the door as if Satan himself were hard on his heels to drag him to hell.

CHAPTER 35

The Assault

The pistol shot awakened Pastor Peter from his trauma as if a giant hand had shaken him from a vivid nightmare. He became aware of his urine-soaked underwear, the intense throbbing heartbeat in his right hand, and the blood, which continued to well up around the round shard of glass embedded in and through the fleshy area of his palm below his thumb. He felt he was about to faint and just before he passed out he vomited up the wine he had drunk. This sobered him and he heard the screech of tires in the church parking lot as Ted's Cadillac left at high speed. Peter crawled to the telephone on his knees, steadying himself with his left arm, and once he reached it, using his left hand he dialed 911.

Ted's fingers clenched the steering wheel in a death grip, weaving from side to side as he bulled the heavy Cadillac down the road. The speedometer

needle hit seventy-five but Ted paid it no attention. He was repeating his personal mantra as he drove.

"A life without values . . ."

He almost missed a sharp curve and the right front wheel slipped off the asphalt and onto the soft shoulder. He jerked the steering wheel to the left and with an effort regained the paved surface. He continued the mantra.

"ain't worth living."

Ted continued his muttering switching to the opening lines of Psalm 27.

"The Lord is my light and my salvation: whom shall I fear. When the wicked, even mine enemies came upon me to eat up my flesh, they stumbled and fell."

Still reciting Psalm 27, Ted's Cadillac sped by George Jackson's home, screamed up the gravel driveway, onto the grass and into Little Souls cemetery mowing down dozens of the miniature white crosses until it slammed into two granite headstones belonging to George's ancestors. The impact threw Ted, who never fastened his seat belt as he regarded them as just one more liberal government infringement on his freedom, into the steering wheel, the blow to his forehead momentarily stunned him. The headstones cracked in two and the trunk of the car popped open. Ted shook his head, which showed only a slight laceration above his right eye. The wind was temporarily knocked out of him as his chest had impacted the lower half of the wheel and when he took his first deep breath he thought he might have cracked a rib or two but paid no attention. He opened the door and nearly fell but managed to stagger to his feet. In the trunk of the car he kept a large, red metal, five-gallon Eagle gas can filled with high-octane fuel. Seized with an overwhelming desire for vengeance on all his perceived enemies and seeing expiation and final victory within his grasp, Ted lifted the heavy can as if it were empty. He weaved in and out of the remaining upright crosses carefully anointing each one with small measures of gas as he walked all through the cemetery. Surveying his work and finding it thorough and satisfactory, he removed a kitchen match from his khaki coat pocket and struck it on a nearby granite tombstone and cast it on the nearest soaked white cross. Within seconds it seemed all Little Souls was ablaze.

Elated by his success, Ted walked to the abandoned slave shack, which George and Stevie used for storage of graveyard tools and other maintenance necessities. He grabbed a heavy mattock and set it outside. Then he poured gasoline on the rotted but dried-out wood floor until it was thoroughly soaked. He stepped outside, struck a match and threw it through the open door. Bright orange flames leapt up and engulfed the interior. Ted shouldered the mattock and walked toward the graves of George's ancestors.

George had heard the strange sound of Ted's Cadillac crashing into his forebears' tombstones but he was tired and thought whatever caused it could wait until morning but by then the flames from the conflagration engulfing the entire cemetery flickered in his room like lightning at which point he roused himself and dressed quickly. George opened the door to the strangest and most unnerving sight he had ever seen. Every cross in Little Souls seemed to be alight and this conjured up images of the Klan and the nightriders that so terrified earlier generations of Jacksons in far southern Tennessee. In the midst of this modern day Walpurgis-night, with unbelieving eyes, George saw Ted Sanders knocking over Jackson headstones with his mattock breaking off large chunks with each wild swing. He had succeeded in partially destroying two, one belonging to George's mother and was lifting the mattock to strike another when George ran out of his house with all the blankets he could carry, shouting at the top of his lungs.

"What are you doing . . . NO!"

George made a futile attempt to smother the flames consuming a few of the Little Souls crosses as Ted continued to swing furiously at George's

grandfather's headstone, the mattock struck sparks as it smashed against the simple granite marker. As frantic as he was, George had no intention of getting in range of the wildly swinging tool Ted was wielding.

Though she was having a not unpleasant dream, Stevie sensed something was badly wrong and she got up, put on a thick cotton robe and looked out the trailer's window and saw Little Souls burning.

"Oh my God!"

She flew to Gigi's room only to find her daughter sitting up and looking at her with bright, brown eyes. Stevie barked,

"Gigi, Stay right here! Do not get out of bed. Mommy will be right back."

Stevie should have known such instructions delivered without a full explanation of the reason for their issuance to a lively, intelligent, five year old only increases her or his curiosity, ensuring that the instructions will not be followed but guaranteeing the exact opposite will be obeyed.

After successfully beating down two fires, George suddenly felt like a hundred pound weight was placed on the left side of his chest. His heart was racing and he struggled to take a breath. Sweat broke out over his entire body and the sensation of having an elephant's foot on his chest drove him to his knees, heedless of the conflagration surrounding him. Ted was exhausted by his mattock work and hurled it to the ground. As he turned, he saw George crumple to the ground dangerously close to a burning cross. Even through the miasmatic mania clouding his thoughts he knew George was having a cardiac episode as his face was contorted in agony and he was hugging his chest with his arms. Ted had seen his father collapse, stricken suddenly by the heart attack that killed him. Without thinking that the figure on the ground was a black man named George and for the moment forgetting his lifelong disdain for him and hatred for the entire long dead Jackson family, Ted only saw a man like his father in serious trouble. He ran to George just as the right cuff of George's pants caught fire. Ted beat out the fire with his bare hands and heedless of his burns, dragged George out of harm's way as the fires continued to rage.

Stevie was frantic with worry, terror, and confusion as she reached them. Her first concern was George. She cried,

"George! George!"

She turned from George to her father and screamed.

"What are you doing?"

Ted knew a heart attack when he saw one. He put his hands on his daughter's shoulders and turned her away from the stricken George.

"Listen to me girl! Go call 911! Now!'

Stevie stood unable to move. The entire scene had temporarily paralyzed her. She was in a living nightmare as if something indescribably evil were chasing her and her feet were glued to the earth. Ted shouted and then he shoved her in the direction of the trailer.

"Go on girl! Get!"

Stevie obeyed, just as she had decades earlier when Ted killed the raccoon. She shook off her paralysis, turned, and ran headlong to her trailer. Now it was Ted who stood still, dazed and nearly unconscious though he was upright. Lying on the ground at full length, George raised himself on his elbows and said in a pathetically weak voice, almost in a whisper:

"Ted."

When Stevie reached her trailer she was breathing hard, her own heart racing, and though she was nauseated she frantically phoned 911. Ted gazed at the trailer-reflected flames dancing on its polished aluminum side and he saw Gigi's face in the window, staring out at what was happening to Little Souls with wide-eyed wonder. He then looked down at George and over at Stevie who was standing in the trailer's doorway, cellphone to her ear, tears streaming down her face. Something that seemed long overdue snapped in Ted's mind and it was instantly filled with a crystal clear, irresistible

command. He thought it was coming straight from the Lord to him as a revelation. Ted spoke aloud but it was not his previous mantra. It was a transcendent vision. Not only was God's voice within him but he could also see a clearly a path to eternal salvation. The path was just so incredibly obvious, so close, so beautiful, and so easily walked. It was far more immediate and logical to him than any path offered by any of the verses in the Bible he had been devouring so zealously with Pastor Peter in the years prior to his receiving the fateful photo.

"Laura. Laura my love, I'm coming. I'm coming."

The cemetery was as light as day. Despite his own agonizing chest pain George could see a sort of divine madness take Ted and he knew that his lifelong antagonist had lost all contact with reality and what he was about to do. He screamed as loudly as he was able but his cry was faint.

"Ted no. Don't do it!"

The voice in Ted's head was infinitely louder and more compelling than George's and he had no more choice to obey it than Moses had to listen to the burning bush. Ted began to walk slowly and inexorably toward the slave shack that incredibly was still standing despite being fully engulfed. George screamed as loudly as he was able, the pressure in his chest having diminished slightly.

"Ted! Don't do it! Please don't! STOP!"

Ted was now within a few feet of the shack, oblivious of the searing heat and impervious to George's repeated cries. Stevie was racing back to comfort George while she waited for the ambulance. As she threw herself on the ground next to George, she remembered her father.

"Where is he? Where did he go?"

George wordlessly pointed to the slave shack as Ted stood still for a moment staring into the burning interior. Stevie uttered a piercing cry.

"No. No!"

Then Ted walked through the flaming open door as calmly if he were Shadrach sitting in Nebuchadnezzar's furnace. Stevie stood up and was about to run after him but George sat up and grabbed her by the knees using what strength remained to restrain her.

"No. Stevie! It's too late."

The roof of the shack caved in and the sides collapsed in an dramatic eruption of flame as showers of sparks and embers flew upward. Stevie shrieked.

"Noooooooo! Daddy!"

Then she fell stunned and senseless into George's arms as limp as one of Gigi's well-worn rag dolls.

CHAPTER 36

Aftermath

For weeks afterward Little Souls resembled a Dresden in miniature following the allied firebombing. Five gallons of Speedway 93 octane had utterly transformed the cemetery. Prior to his self-immolation, despite his unbalanced state of mind, Ted Sanders had been remarkably thorough, judicious, and thoughtful in applying his five gallons to the crosses and slave shack. The trunks of the old oak trees were charred, and much of the grass was shriveled and blackened. Many of the hundreds of crosses were either partially or wholly consumed. Only ashes remained of the slave shack and the Zion County coroner had carefully sifted them in order to preserve what little remained of Ted.

Stevie stood amid the ruins, mallet in hand, tapping a new little white cross into the earth at the head of a tiny grave. George sat quietly in a wheelchair with Faith's shawl draped over his knees. A folding table with a plastic top decorated with various species of butterflies was next to him with a coffee cup in easy reach. George was alternating between reading Maya Angelou's "And Still I Rise" and watching Stevie. He counted twenty fresh crosses. He thought that left about two hundred to go. Stevie left off tapping as she heard a truck approach. She did not recognize the somewhat dilapidated, old, white Ford F-350 dually. She was pleasantly surprised to see not only Daniel and Cheryl, but also the sheriff as well all exiting the Ford. Stevie walked over to the three, mallet gently swinging by its leather lanyard from her right hand.

"Hey Daniel, Cheryl."

Here she nodded respectfully to the sheriff.

"Sheriff."

Daniel was smiling broadly.

"Stevie, we thought we'd come and help out."

The four of them moved to the back of the truck, which was loaded with brand new garden tools and bundles of white painted stakes for making Little Souls' signature white crosses and restoring the picket fencing.

The sheriff grinned and touched the brim of his blue-and-gold embroidered county sheriff's ball cap.

"All this is courtesy of Lucille Abbott."

Daniel dropped the tailgate, which groaned due to lack of recent lubrication and some old corrosion. He reached in and grasped a bundle of stakes.

"Best get to work. Only thing sure about the weather hereabouts is that it's bound to change."

Stevie was both deeply touched, confused, and about to burst into tears. She was so used to being the painted bird, the outsider, the weirdo, that she was almost unable to feel so understood, so warmly embraced by the community that had previously categorically rejected both her and

her life's work. She stuttered as she spoke, overcome with emotion, tears standing in her eyes.

"I ... I don't know how to thank you."

Cheryl gave her a warm smile.

"Honey, you don't need to."

The truck bed also contained some completed crosses, which had been assembled by the sheriff in his workshop. Sheriff Olsen looked at Cheryl with warmth and acceptance and handed her one of his crosses.

"Here you go."

Cheryl accepted the cross with a smile of her own and handed it to Stevie. Daniel looked at Stevie.

"So you managed to save George's farm."

Stevie nodded.

"I inherited Sanders Plantation and I worked something out with the bank."

Daniel just smiled at this information, then he, Cheryl, and the sheriff continued unloading bundles of pickets and tools laying them in neat piles. Stevie was about to join in the unloading when she saw Pastor Peter in the plantation house driveway. He had his Adventure MX horse trailer hooked up to his SUV. Stevie excused herself and while the others began work, tools in hand, Stevie walked to the house. Peter carefully climbed out of the SUV, favoring his right hand, which was swathed in a very large bandage. Stevie looked first at the bandage and then at Peter, who looked as if he had not had a full night's sleep for days. His face bore new worry lines and there were bags under his eyes. His skin was unusually sallow and Stevie had never seen him looking so unhealthy even when he had had the flu. For the first time in their relationship she felt a distinct lack of physical attraction to him, so much so it bordered on revulsion. This realization was shocking to her but in another way it was liberating. With considerably more interest and enthusiasm than she actually felt she said,

"Hey you. Where have you been?"

Peter did not embrace her or even extend his hand in greeting. It was evident he was suffering; however she knew whatever pain he was experiencing was completely self-inflicted, a result of his mentoring her father while all the time violating every principle Ted held by his relationship with her. Stevie's feelings were conflicted but she could not help being even further alienated by his apparent coldness.

"I've been thinking and praying for guidance the past few days. I cannot forgive myself for what I did to your father. I've been a very poor pastor and a false friend."

He hesitated and looked pathetically at Stevie.

"In all too many ways."

Stevie answered this apologia rather more sharply than she intended to for this self-flagellation annoyed her.

"But I can forgive you, and I do. What happened to my father wasn't your fault. He did it to himself and eventually would have done something equally self-destructive with or without you."

Peter stood unmoved by her statement. He continued.

"I need to leave the ministry. At least until I can come to terms with what I've done here."

Peter suddenly became wistful and a dreamy quality came over his face transforming him from a sad, suffering, overwrought, and tortured man to the man Stevie had loved.

"Someday I'd like you and Gigi to visit me in Connecticut. It's so beautiful there."

Stevie shook her head emphatically.

"Peter, you know my place is in the South and my work and life are here."

She pointed to George sitting in his wheelchair, which was visible in the distance.

"And so is my family."

This poignant gesture made it abundantly clear to Peter that his fantasy of marrying Stevie was just that and would always remain one. Seeing the hunger in Peter's eyes Stevie softened her tone.

"Peter, regardless of what happens in the future, I swear to you that Gabriella will always know and love you like a father."

They looked at each other for a very long moment and then they moved simultaneously, locked in a tight embrace, though Peter held his right hand out to the side, which rendered the hug slightly awkward.

Peter broke the hug first and was going to kiss Stevie on the lips but she turned her head and this resulted in his kissing her right cheek. She really didn't want an overly demonstrative parting in front of Cheryl, Daniel, and the sheriff though they were some distance away busily replacing crosses. She did not want to admit it to herself but Peter's repeated efforts to force her into an unwanted marriage by relying on her father's biblical arguments, combined with his using Gigi in an effort to extort her acquiescence to his proposals, had so vitiated her romantic feelings for him that the thought of a real kiss with him was repellent to her. She knew it was not his fault but to her it was yet another demonstration of Peter's inherent weakness and that only made her disinclination stronger. He sensed her reluctance and did not look her in the eye as he opened the SUV door with his left hand and favoring his bandaged right, he folded himself into the driver's seat and closed the door. Peter's horse, Traveler, was becoming restless with the lack of movement and stamped his front hoof repeatedly to show his impatience.

As Stevie was berating herself for her lack of powerful emotion at Peter's imminent departure, she thought of Traveler. She loved horses in general and Traveler in particular but deplored Peter's choice of a name. Was he so pedestrian that he named him after Robert E. Lee's famous mount and so unimaginative that he couldn't come up with something original? This was just another example of southern inability to look to the future rather than remain mired in an infamous, even traitorous past. Peter wasn't even from the south so what was he thinking? "Funny," she thought. "I never bothered to ask him about it."

As he was driving away steering with his left hand, Peter twisted himself so he could wave out the window with his right. Stevie looked at the large, white, bandaged hand waving and she felt an irresistible giggle welling up. Peter's hand looked like nothing so much as an enormous Q-tip waving farewell. The last image of Peter she could recall from that day was the top of Traveler's butt, his tail swishing, as it slowly diminished in the distance.

Now that the five-year-long affair had come to its end and the parting was over, a relieved and reinvigorated Stevie walked briskly back to George, who was enjoying all the activity and watching Gigi scamper among the graves picking violets, daisies, and here and there a purple thistle. George smiled broadly.

"She's getting so big."

Stevie laughed.

"Tell me about it."

Gigi ran up brimming with pride and excitement over her exuberantly wild bouquet, which she waved at George and Stevie. The little girl was beaming.

"Wow! Honey who is that for?"

Gigi said matter-of-factly, as if it should be obvious to anyone with a brain in her head:

"Grandpa."

The "of course" was implied in her tone.

The mention of her father no longer caused Stevie the acute bolt of nausea it once always had. She smiled at her daughter.

"Well then. Let's go give them to him."

~ THE END ~